'The deal is subject to a condition?' Diego's expression was coolly aloof.

Cassandra's eyes glittered with barely repressed anger. 'My brother said it was personal. *How* personal?'

'Two separate nights and one weekend with you.'

It took her a few seconds to find her voice. 'I won't have sex with you.'

'You're not in any position to bargain.'

'I'm not for sale,' Cassandra evinced with dignity.

'*Everything* has its price.'

D1142727

Helen Bianchin was born in New Zealand and travelled to Australia before marrying her Italian-born husband. After three years they moved, returned to New Zealand with their daughter, had two sons, then resettled in Australia. Encouraged by friends to recount anecdotes of her years as a tobacco sharefarmer's wife living in an Italian community, Helen began setting words on paper and her first novel was published in 1975. An animal lover, she says her terrier and Persian cat regard her study as much theirs as hers.

Recent titles by the same author:

THE PREGNANCY PROPOSAL
THE GREEK BRIDEGROOM*
A PASSIONATE SURRENDER*
THE WEDDING ULTIMATUM

*linked stories

IN THE SPANIARD'S BED

BY

HELEN BIANCHIN

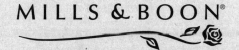

MILLS & BOON®

DID YOU PURCHASE THIS BOOK WITHOUT A COVER?

If you did, you should be aware it is **stolen property** as it was reported *unsold and destroyed* by a retailer. Neither the author nor the publisher has received any payment for this book.

All the characters in this book have no existence outside the imagination of the author, and have no relation whatsoever to anyone bearing the same name or names. They are not even distantly inspired by any individual known or unknown to the author, and all the incidents are pure invention.

All Rights Reserved including the right of reproduction in whole or in part in any form. This edition is published by arrangement with Harlequin Enterprises II B.V. The text of this publication or any part thereof may not be reproduced or transmitted in any form or by any means, electronic or mechanical, including photocopying, recording, storage in an information retrieval system, or otherwise, without the written permission of the publisher.

This book is sold subject to the condition that it shall not, by way of trade or otherwise, be lent, resold, hired out or otherwise circulated without the prior consent of the publisher in any form of binding or cover other than that in which it is published and without a similar condition including this condition being imposed on the subsequent purchaser.

MILLS & BOON and MILLS & BOON with the Rose Device are registered trademarks of the publisher.

*First published in Great Britain 2003
Harlequin Mills & Boon Limited,
Eton House, 18-24 Paradise Road, Richmond, Surrey TW9 1SR*

© Helen Bianchin 2003

ISBN 0 263 83314 3

*Set in Times Roman 10½ on 12 pt.
01-0903-37658*

*Printed and bound in Spain
by Litografía Rosés, S.A., Barcelona*

CHAPTER ONE

'I'M ON my way.' Cassandra released the intercom, caught up her evening purse, keys, exited her apartment and took the lift down to the foyer where her brother was waiting.

At twenty-nine he was two years her senior, and he shared her blond hair, fair skin and blue eyes. Average height in comparison to her petite frame.

'Wow,' Cameron complimented with genuine admiration, and she responded with an affectionate smile.

'Brotherly love, huh?'

The ice-pink gown moulded her slender curves, its spaghetti straps showing silky skin to an advantage, and the diagonal ruffled split to mid-thigh showcased beautifully proportioned legs. A gossamer wrap in matching ice-pink completed the outfit, and her jewellery was understated.

'Seriously cool.'

She tilted her head to one side as she tucked a hand through his arm. 'Let's go slay the masses.'

Tonight's fundraiser was a prestigious event whose guests numbered among Sydney's social élite. Held in the ballroom of a prominent city hotel, it was one of several annual soirées Cassandra and her brother attended on their father's behalf after a heart attack and stroke two years ago forced him into early retirement.

Guests were mingling in the large foyer when they arrived, and she summoned a practised smile as she acknowledged a few acquaintances, pausing to exchange a greeting with one friend or another as she selected iced water from a hovering drinks waiter.

Observing the social niceties was something she did well. Private schooling and a finishing year in France had added polish and panache. The Preston-Villers family held a certain social standing of which her father was justly proud.

While Cameron had been groomed to enter the Preston-Villers conglomerate from an early age, Cassandra chose to pursue gemmology and jewellery design, added the necessary degree, studied with a well-known jeweller and she was now beginning to gain a reputation for her work.

Mixing and mingling was part of the social game, and she did it well.

Committee members conferred and worked the room in a bid to ensure the evening's success. The hotel ballroom was geared to seat a thousand guests, and it was rumoured there had been a waiting list for last-minute ticket cancellations.

'There's something I need to discuss with you.'

Cassandra met Cameron's gaze, examined his expression, and restrained a faint frown as she glimpsed the slight edginess apparent.

'Here, now?' she queried lightly, and waited for his usual carefree smile.

'Later.'

It couldn't be anything serious, she dismissed, otherwise he would have mentioned it during the drive in to the city.

'Darling, how are you?'

The soft feminine purr evoked a warm smile as she turned to greet the tall, slender model. 'Siobhan.' Her eyes sparkled. They'd attended the same school, shared much, and were firm friends. 'I'm fine, and you?'

'Flying out to Rome tomorrow, then it's Milan followed by Paris.'

Cassandra uttered a subdued chuckle in amusement. 'It's a hard life.'

Siobhan grinned. 'But an interesting one,' she conceded. 'I have a date with an Italian count in Rome.'

'Ah.'

'Old money, and *divine*.'

The musing twinkle in those gorgeous green eyes brought forth a husky laugh as Cassandra shook her head. 'You're wicked.'

'This time it's serious,' Siobhan declared as Cassandra's smile widened.

'It always is.'

'Got to go. The parents are in tow.'

'Have fun.'

'I shall. In Italy.' She leaned forward and pressed her cheek against Cassandra's in a gesture of affection.

'Take care.'

'Always.'

Soon the ballroom doors would be open, and guests would be called to take their seats. There would be the introductory and explanatory speeches, the wine stewards would do their thing, and the first course served.

Speaking of which, she was hungry. Lunch had been yoghurt and fruit snatched between the usual weekend chores.

Cameron appeared deep in conversation with a man she presumed to be a business associate, and she sipped chilled water from her glass as she debated whether to join him.

At that moment she felt the warning prickle of awareness as her senses went on alert, and she let her gaze skim the guests.

There was only one man who had this particular effect on her equilibrium.

Innate instinct? An elusive knowledge based on the inexplicable?

Whatever, it was crazy. Maddening.

Maybe this time she had it wrong. Although all it took was one glance at that familiar dark head to determine her instinct was right on target.

Diego del Santo. Successful entrepreneur, one of the city's nouveau riche…and her personal nemesis.

Born in New York of Spanish immigrant parents, it was reported he'd lived in the wrong part of town, fought for survival in the streets, and made his money early, so it was rumoured, by means beyond legitimate boundaries of the law.

He took risks, it was said, no sensible man would touch. Yet those risks had paid off a million-fold several times over. Literally.

In idle fascination she watched as he turned towards her, then he murmured something to his companion and slowly closed the distance between them.

'Cassandra.'

The voice was low, impossibly deep with the barest trace of an accent, and possessed of the power to send tiny shivers feathering the length of her spine.

Tall, broad-framed, with the sculptured facial features of his Spanish ancestors. Dark, well-groomed hair, dark, almost black eyes, and a mouth that promised a thousand delights.

A mouth that had briefly tasted her own when she'd disobeyed her father and persuaded Cameron to take her to a party. Sixteen years old, emerging hormones, a sense of the forbidden combined with a desire to play grown-up had proved a volatile mix. Add her brother with his own agenda, a few sips too many of wine, a young man who seemed intent on leading her astray, and she could easily have been in over her head. Except Diego del Santo had materialised out of nowhere, intervened, read her the Riot Act, then proceeded to show her precisely what she should be wary of when she heedlessly chose to flirt. Within minutes he had summoned Cameron and she found herself bundled into her brother's car and driven home.

Eleven years had passed since that fateful episode, ten of which Diego had spent in his native New York creating his fortune.

Yet she possessed a vivid recollection of how it felt to have his mouth savour her own. The electric primitiveness of his touch, almost as if he had reached down to her soul and staked a claim.

Diego del Santo had projected a raw quality that meshed leashed savagery with blatant sensuality. A dangerously compelling mix, and one that attracted females from fifteen to fifty.

Now there were no rough edges, and he bore the mantle of power with the same incredible ease he wore his designer clothes.

In his mid-to-late thirties, Diego del Santo was a seriously rich man whose property investments and developments formed a financial portfolio that edged him close to billionaire status.

As such, his return to Australia a year ago had soon seen him become an A-list member of Sydney's social élite, receiving invitations to each and every soirée of note. His acceptance was selective, and his donations to worthy charities, legend.

Preston-Villers' involvement with similar charity events and her father's declining health meant they were frequently fellow guests at one function or another. It was something she accepted, and dealt with by presenting a polite façade.

Only she knew the effect he had on her. The way her pulse jumped and thudded to a rapid beat. No one could possibly be aware her stomach curled into a painful knot at the mere sight of him, or how one glance at his sensual mouth heated the blood in her veins in a vivid reminder of the way it felt to have that mouth possess her own.

The slow sweep of his tongue, the promise of passion, the gentle, coaxing quality that caught her tentative response and took it to an undreamt-of dimension.

Eleven years. Yet his kiss was hauntingly vivid…a taunting example by which she'd unconsciously measured each kiss that followed it. None matched up, no matter how hard she tried to convince herself imagination had merely enhanced the memory.

There were occasions when she thought she should dispense with her own curiosity and accept one of his many invitations. Yet each time something held her back, an innate knowledge such a step would put her way out of her depth.

His invitations and her refusals had become something akin to a polite game they each played. What would he do, she mused, if she surprised him by accepting?

Are you *insane?* a tiny voice queried insidiously.

'Diego,' Cassandra acknowledged coolly, meeting his compelling gaze with equanimity, watching as he inclined his head to her brother.

'Cameron.'

For a millisecond she thought she glimpsed some unspoken signal pass between the men, then she dismissed it as fanciful.

'A successful evening, wouldn't you agree?'

Tonight's event was a charity fundraiser aiding state-of-the-art equipment for a special wing of the city's children's hospital.

Without doubt there were a number of guests with a genuine interest in the nominated charity. However, the majority viewed the evening as a glitz-and-glamour function at which the women would attempt to outdo each other with designer gowns and expensive jewellery, whilst the men wheeled and dealed beneath the guise of socialising.

Diego del Santo didn't fit easily into any recognisable category.

Not that she had any interest in pigeon-holing him. In fact, she did her best to pretend he didn't exist. Something he seemed intent on proving otherwise.

He could have any woman he wanted. And probably did. His photo graced the social pages of numerous newspapers and magazines, inevitably with a stunning female glued to his side.

There was a primitive quality evident. A hint of something dangerous beneath the surface should anyone dare to consider scratching it.

A man who commanded respect and admiration in the boardroom. Possessed of the skill, so it was whispered, and the passion to drive a woman wild in the bedroom.

It was a dramatic mesh of elemental ruthlessness and latent sensuality. Lethal.

Some women would excel at the challenge of taming him, enjoying the ride for however long it lasted. But she wasn't one of them. Only a fool ventured into the devil's playground with the hope they wouldn't get burnt.

Eluding Diego was a game she became adept at playing. If they happened to meet, she offered a polite smile, acknowledged his presence, then moved on.

Yet their social schedule was such, those occasions were many. If she didn't know better, she could almost swear he was intent on playing a game of his own.

'If you'll excuse me,' Cassandra ventured. 'There's someone I should catch up with.' A timeworn phrase, trite but true, for there were always a few friends she could greet by way of escape.

Cameron wanted to protest, she could tell, although Diego del Santo merely inclined his head.

Which didn't help at all, for she could *feel* those dark eyes watching her as she moved away.

Sensation feathered the length of her spine, and something tugged deep inside in a vivid reminder of the effect he had on her composure.

Get over it, she chided silently as she deliberately sought a cluster of friends and blended seamlessly into their conversation.

Any time soon the doors into the ballroom would open and guests would be encouraged to take their seats at designated tables. Then she could rejoin Cameron, and prepare to enjoy the evening.

'You had no need to disappear,' Cameron chastised as she moved to his side.

'Diego del Santo might be serious eye candy, but he's not my type.'

'No?'

'No.' She managed a smile, held it, and began threading her way towards their table.

'Do you know who else is joining us?' Cassandra queried lightly as she slid into one of four remaining seats, and took time to greet the six guests already seated.

'Here they are now.'

She registered Cameron's voice, glanced up from the table…and froze.

Diego del Santo and the socialite and model, Alicia Vandernoot.

No. The silent scream seemed to echo inside her head.

It was bad enough having to acknowledge his presence and converse for a few minutes. To have to share a table with him for the space of an evening was way too much!

Had Cameron organised this? She wanted to rail against him and demand *Why?* Except there wasn't the opportunity to do so without drawing unwanted attention.

If Diego chose the chair next to hers, she'd scream!

Of course he did. It was one of the correct dictums of society when it came to seating arrangements. Although she had little doubt he enjoyed the irony.

Cassandra murmured a polite greeting, and her faint smile was a mere facsimile.

This close she was far too aware of him, the clean smell of freshly laundered clothes, the subtle aroma of his exclusive cologne.

Yet it was the man himself, his potent masculinity and the sheer primitive force he exuded that played havoc with her senses.

A few hours, she consoled herself silently. All she had to do was sip wine, eat the obligatory three courses set in front of her, and make polite conversation. She could manage that, surely?

Not so easy, Cassandra acknowledged as she displayed intent interest in the charity chairperson's introduction prior to revealing funding endeavours, results and expectations.

Every nerve in her body was acutely attuned to Diego del Santo, supremely conscious of each move he made.

'More water?'

He had topped up Alicia's goblet, and now offered to refill her own.

'No, thank you.' Her goblet was part-empty, but she'd be damned if she'd allow him to tend to her.

Did he sense her reaction? Probably. He was too astute not to realise her excruciating politeness indicated she didn't want anything to do with him.

Uniformed waiters delivered starters with practised efficiency, and she forked the artistically arranged food without appetite.

'The seafood isn't to your satisfaction?'

His voice was an accented drawl tinged with amusement, and she met his dark gaze with equanimity, almost inclined to offer a negation just to see what he'd do, aware he'd probably summon the waiter and insist on a replacement.

'Yes.'

The single affirmative surprised her, and she deliberately widened her eyes. 'You read minds?'

The edge of his mouth curved, and there was a humorous gleam apparent. 'It's one of my talents.'

Cassandra deigned not to comment, and deliberately turned her attention to the contents on her plate, unsure if she heard his faint, husky chuckle or merely imagined it.

He was the most irritating, impossible man she'd

ever met. Examining why wasn't on her agenda. At least that's what she told herself whenever Diego's image intruded…on far too many occasions for her peace of mind.

It was impossible to escape the man. He was *there,* a constant in the media, cementing another successful business deal, escorting a high-profile female personality to one social event or another. Cameron accorded him an icon, and mentioned him frequently in almost reverent tones.

Tonight Diego del Santo had chosen to invade her personal space. Worse, she had little option but to remain in his immediate proximity for a few hours, and she resented his manipulation, hated him for singling her out as an object for his amusement.

For that was all it was…and it didn't help that she felt like a butterfly pinned to the wall.

Cassandra took a sip of wine, and deliberately engaged Cameron in conversation, the thread of which she lost minutes later as the waiter removed plates from their table.

She was supremely conscious of Diego's proximity, the shape of his hand as he reached for his wine goblet, the way his fingers curved over the delicate glass…and couldn't stop the wayward thought as to how his hands would glide over a woman's skin.

Where had that come from?

Dear heaven, the wine must have affected her

brain! The last thing she wanted was any physical contact with a man of Diego del Santo's ilk.

'Your speciality is gemmology, I believe?'

Think of the devil and he speaks, she alluded with silent cynicism as she turned towards him. 'Polite conversation, genuine interest,' she inclined, and waited a beat. 'Or an attempt to alleviate boredom?'

His expression didn't change, although she could have sworn something moved in the depths of those dark eyes. 'Let's aim for the middle ground.'

There was a quality to his voice, an inflexion she preferred to ignore. 'Natural precious gemstones recovered in the field by mining or fossiking techniques are the most expensive.' Such facts were common knowledge. 'For a jewellery designer, they give more pleasure to work with, given there's a sense of nature and the process of their existence. It becomes a personal challenge to have the stones cut in such a way they display maximum beauty. The designer's gift to ensure the design and setting reflect the stone's optimal potential.' A completed study of gemmology had led to her true passion of jewellery design.

Diego saw the way her mouth softened and her eyes came alive. It intrigued him, as *she* intrigued him.

'You are not in favour of the synthetic or simulants?'

Her expression faded a little. 'They're immensely popular and have a large market.'

His gaze held hers. 'That doesn't answer the question.' He lifted a hand and fingered the delicate argyle diamond nestling against the hollow at the base of her throat. 'Your work?' It was a rhetorical question. He'd made it his business to view her designs, without her knowledge, and was familiar with each and every one of them.

She flinched at his touch, hating his easy familiarity almost as much as she hated the tell-tale warmth flooding her veins.

If she could, she'd have flung the icy contents of her glass in his face. Instead, she forced her voice to remain calm. 'Yes.'

A woman could get lost in the depths of those dark eyes, for there was warm sensuality lurking just beneath the surface, a hint, a promise, of the delights he could provide.

Sensation feathered the length of her spine, and she barely repressed a shiver at the thought of his mouth on hers, the touch of his hands…how it would feel to be driven wild, beyond reason, by such a man.

'Have dinner with me tomorrow night.'

'The obligatory invitation?' Her response was automatic, and she tempered it with a gracious, 'Thank you. No.'

The edge of his mouth lifted. 'The obligatory refusal…because you have to wash your hair?'

'I can come up with something more original.'

She could, easily. Except she doubted an excuse, no matter how legitimate-sounding, would fool him.

'You won't change your mind?'

Cassandra offered a cool smile. 'What part of *no* don't you understand?'

Diego reached for the water jug and refilled her glass. The sleeve of his jacket brushed her arm, and her stomach turned a slow somersault at the contact.

It was as well the waiters began delivering the main course, and she sipped wine in the hope it would soothe her nerves.

Chance would be a fine thing! She was conscious of every move he made, aware of the restrained power beneath the fine Armani tailoring, the dangerous aura he seemed to project without any effort at all.

Another two hours. Three at the most. Then she could excuse herself and leave. If Cameron wanted to stay on, she'd take a cab home.

Cassandra drew a calming breath and regarded the contents on her plate. The meal was undoubtedly delicious, but her appetite had vanished.

With determined effort she caught Cameron's attention, and deliberately sought his opinion on something so inconsequential that afterwards she had little recollection of the discussion.

There were the usual speeches, followed by light entertainment as dessert and coffee were served. Never had time dragged quite so slowly, nor could she recall an occasion when she'd so badly wanted the evening to end.

To her surprise, it was Cameron who initiated the desire to leave, citing a headache as the reason, and Cassandra rose to her feet, offered a polite good-night to the occupants of their table, then preceded her brother out to the foyer.

'Are you OK?'

He looked pale, too pale, and a slight frown creased her brow as they headed towards the bank of lifts. 'Headache?' She extended her hand as he retrieved his car keys. 'Want me to drive?'

CHAPTER TWO

MINUTES later she slid behind the wheel and sent the car up to street level to join the flow of traffic. It was a beautiful night, the air crisp and cool indicative of spring.

A lovely time of year, she accorded silently as she negotiated lanes and took the route that led to Double Bay.

Fifteen, twenty minutes tops, and she'd be home. Then she could get out of the formal gear, cleanse off her make-up, and slip into bed.

'We need to talk.'

Cassandra spared him a quick glance. 'Can't it wait until tomorrow?'

'No.'

It was most unlike Cameron to be taciturn. 'Is something wrong?' Her eyes narrowed as the car in front came to a sudden stop, and she uttered an unladylike curse as she stamped her foot hard on the brakes.

'Hell, Cassandra,' he muttered. 'Watch it!'

'Tell that to the guy in front.' Her voice held unaccustomed vehemence. Choosing silence for the remaining time it took to reach her apartment seemed a wise option. The last thing she coveted was an argument.

'Park in the visitors' bay,' Cameron instructed as she swept the car into the bricked apron adjacent to the main entrance.

'You're coming up?'

'It's either that, or we talk in the car.'

He didn't seem to be giving her a choice as he unbuckled his seat belt and slid out from the passenger seat.

She followed, inserted her personalised card into the security slot to gain entry into the foyer, and used it again to summon a lift.

'I hope this won't take long,' she cautioned as she preceded him into her apartment, then she turned to face him. 'OK, shoot.'

He closed his eyes, then opened them again and ran a hand through his hair. 'This isn't easy.'

The tension of the evening began to manifest itself into tiredness, and she rolled her shoulders. 'Just spit it out.'

'The firm is in trouble. Major financial trouble,' he elaborated. 'If Dad found out just how hopeless everything is, it would kill him.'

Ice crept towards the region of her heart. 'What in hell are you talking about?'

'Preston-Villers is on a roller-coaster ride to insolvency.'

'What?' She found it difficult to comprehend. *'How?'*

He was ready to crumple, and it wasn't a good look.

'Bad management, bad deals, unfulfilled contracts. Staff problems. You name it, it happened.'

She adored her brother, but he wasn't the son her father wanted. Cameron didn't possess the steel backbone, the unflagging determination to take over directorship of Preston-Villers. Their father had thought it would be the making of his son. Now it appeared certain to be his ruination.

'Just how bad is it?'

Cameron grimaced, and shot her a desperate look. 'The worst.' He held up a hand. 'Yes, I've done the round of banks, financiers, sought independent advice.' He drew in a deep breath and released it slowly. 'It narrows down to two choices. Liquidate, or take a conditional offer.'

Hope was uppermost, and she ran with it. 'The offer is legitimate?'

'Yes.' He rubbed a weary hand along his jaw. 'An investor is prepared to inject the necessary funds, I get to retain an advisory position, he brings in his professional team, shares joint directorship, and takes a half-share of all profits.'

It sounded like salvation, but there was need for caution. 'Presumably you've taken legal advice on all this?'

'It's the only deal in town,' he assured soberly. 'There's just a matter of the remaining condition.'

'Which is?'

He hesitated, then took a deep breath and expelled it. 'You.'

Genuine puzzlement brought forth a frown. 'The deal has nothing to do with me.'

'Yes, it does.'

Like pieces of a puzzle, they began clicking into place, forming a picture she didn't want to see. 'Who made the offer?' Dear God, no. It couldn't be…

'Diego del Santo.'

Cassandra felt the blood drain from her face. Shock, disbelief, anger followed in quick succession. 'You can't be serious?' The words held a hushed quality, and for a few seconds she wondered if she'd actually uttered them.

Cameron drew in a deep breath, then released it slowly. 'Deadly.' To his credit, Cameron looked wretched.

'Let me get this straight.' Her eyes assumed an icy gleam. 'Diego del Santo intends making this personal?' His image conjured itself in front of her, filling her vision, blinding her with it.

'Without your involvement, the deal won't go ahead.'

She tried for *calm,* when inside she was a seething mass of anger. 'My *involvement* being?'

'He'll discuss it with you over dinner tomorrow evening.'

'The *hell* he will!'

'Cassandra—' Cameron's features assumed a

grey tinge. 'You want Alexander to have another heart attack?'

The words stopped her cold. The medics had warned a further attack could be his last. 'How can you even say that?'

She wanted to rail against him, demand why he'd let things progress beyond the point of no return. Yet recrimination wouldn't solve a thing, except provide a vehicle to vent her feelings.

'I want proof.' The words were cool, controlled. 'Facts,' she elaborated, and glimpsed Cameron's obvious discomfiture. 'The how and why of it, and just how bad it is.'

'You don't believe me?'

'I need to be aware of all the angles,' she elaborated. 'Before I confront Diego del Santo.'

Cameron went a paler shade of pale. 'Confront?'

She fired him a look that quelled him into silence. 'If he thinks I'll meekly comply with whatever he has in mind, then he can think again!'

His mouth worked as he searched for the appropriate words. 'Cass—'

'Don't *Cass* me.' It was an endearing nickname that belonged to their childhood.

'Do you have any idea who you're dealing with?'

She drew in a deep breath and released it slowly. 'I think it's about time Diego del Santo discovered who *he* is dealing with!' She pressed fingers to her throbbing temples in order to ease the ache there.

'Cassandra—'

'Can we leave this until tomorrow?' She needed to *think*. Most of all, she wanted to be alone. 'I'll organise lunch, and we'll go through the paperwork together.'

'It's Sunday.'

'What does that have to do with it?'

Cameron lifted both hands in a gesture of conciliation. 'Midday?'

'Fine.'

She saw him out the door, locked up, then she removed her make-up, undressed, then slid into bed to stare at the darkened ceiling for what seemed an age, sure hours later when she woke that she hadn't slept at all.

A session in the gym, followed by several laps of the pool eased some of her tension, and she re-entered her apartment, showered and dressed in jeans and a loose top, then crossed into the kitchen to prepare lunch.

Cameron arrived at twelve, and presented her with a chilled bottle of champagne.

'A little premature, don't you think?' she offered wryly as she prepared garlic bread and popped it into the oven to heat.

'Something smells good,' he complimented, and she wrinkled her nose at him.

'Flattery won't get you anywhere.' Lunch was a seafood pasta dish she whipped up without any fuss, and accompanied by a fresh garden salad it was an adequate meal.

'Let's eat first, then we'll deal with business. OK?'

He didn't look much better than she felt, and she wondered if he'd slept any more than she had.

'Dad is expecting us for dinner.'

It was a weekly family tradition, and one they observed almost without fail. Although the thought of presenting a false façade didn't sit well. Her father might suffer ill-health, but he wasn't an easy man to fool.

'This pasta is superb,' Cameron declared minutes later, and she inclined her head in silent acknowledgement.

By tacit agreement they discussed everything except Preston-Villers, and it was only when the dishes were dealt with that Cassandra indicated Cameron's briefcase.

'Let's begin, shall we?'

It was worse, much worse than she had envisaged as she perused the paperwork tabling Preston-Villers slide into irretrievable insolvency. The accountant's overview of the current situation was damning, and equally indisputable.

She'd wanted proof. Now she had it.

'I can think of several questions,' she began, but only one stood out. 'Why did you let things get this bad?'

Cameron raked fingers through his hair. 'I kept hoping the contracts would come in and everything would improve.'

Instead, they'd gone from bad to worse.

Cassandra damned Diego del Santo to hell and back, and barely drew short of including Cameron with him.

'Business doesn't succeed on *hope*.' It needed a hard, competent hand holding the reins, taking control, making the right decisions.

A man like Diego del Santo, a quiet voice insisted. Someone who could inject essential funds, and ensure everything ran like well-oiled clockwork.

There was sense in the amalgamation, and as Cameron rightly described, it was the only deal in town if Preston-Villers was to survive.

'Shall I contact Diego and confirm you've reconsidered his dinner invitation?'

'No.'

Disbelief and consternation were clearly evident.

'No?'

'My ball. My play.' Something she intended to take care of tomorrow. She stood to her feet. 'I need to put in an hour or two on the laptop before leaving to have dinner with Dad.' She led the way to the door of her apartment. 'I'll see you there.'

'OK.' Cameron offered an awkward smile. 'Thanks.'

'For what?' She couldn't help herself. 'Lunch?'

'That, too.'

It was after five when Cassandra entered the electronic gates guarding Alexander Preston-Villers' splendid home. Renovations accommodated wheelchair usage, and a lift had been installed for easy access between upper and lower floors. There was a resident housekeeper, as well as Sylvie, the live-in nurse.

Cassandra rang the bell, then used her key to enter the marble-tiled lobby.

It tore at Cassandra's heart each time she visited, seeing the man who had once been strong reduced to frail health.

Tonight he appeared more frail than usual, his lack of motor-skills more pronounced than they had been a week ago, and his appetite seemed less.

She looked at him, and wanted to weep. Cameron seemed similarly affected, and attempting to maintain a normal façade took considerable effort.

There was no way she'd allow *anyone* to upset Alexander. Not Cameron, nor Diego del Santo.

She made the silent vow as she drove back to her apartment. The determined bid haunted her sleep, providing dreams that assumed nightmarish proportions, ensuring she woke late and had to scramble in order to get to work on time.

Confronting Diego del Santo was a priority, and given a choice she'd prefer to beard him in his office than meet socially over a shared meal.

Which meant she'd need to work through her lunch hour in order to leave an hour early.

Cassandra found it difficult to focus on the intricate attention to detail involved with the creative-design project for an influential client.

Diego del Santo's image intruded, wreaking havoc with her concentration, and consequently it was something of a relief to pack up her work and consign it to the security safe before freshening her make-up prior to leaving for the day.

Del Santo Corporation was situated on a high floor of an inner-city office tower, and Cassandra felt a sense of angry determination as she vacated the lift and walked through automatic sliding glass doors to Reception.

'Diego del Santo.' Her voice was firm, clipped and, she hoped, authoritative.

'Mr del Santo is in conference, and has no appointments available this afternoon.'

She made a point of checking her watch. 'Put a call through and tell him Cassandra Preston-Villers is waiting to see him.'

'I have instructions to hold all calls.'

Efficiency. She could only admire it. 'Call his secretary.'

A minute…Cassandra counted off the seconds…a woman who could easily win secretary-of-the-year award appeared in Reception. 'Is there a problem?'

You betcha, Cassandra accorded silently, and I'm it. 'Please inform Diego del Santo I need to see him.'

A flicker of doubt. That's all she needed. Yet none appeared. Was his secretary so familiar with Diego's paramours, she knew categorically that Cassandra wasn't one of them?

'I have instructions to serve drinks and canapés at five,' his secretary informed. 'I'll mention your presence to him then.'

It was a small victory, but a victory none the less. 'Thank you.'

Half an hour spent leafing through a variety of glossy magazines did little to help her nervous tension.

Staff began their end-of-day exodus, and she felt her stomach execute a painful somersault as Diego's secretary moved purposely into Reception.

'Please come with me.'

Minutes later she was shown into a luxurious suite. 'Take a seat. Mr del Santo will be with you soon.'

How soon was *soon?*

Five, ten, thirty minutes passed. Was he playing a diabolical game with her?

Nervous tension combined with anger, and she was almost on the point of walking out. The only thing that stopped her was the sure knowledge she'd only have to go through this again tomorrow.

Five more minutes, she vowed, then she'd go in search of him…conference be damned!

The door swung open and Diego walked into the room with one minute to spare.

'Cassandra.'

She rose to her feet, unwilling to appear at a disadvantage by having him loom over her.

'My apologies for keeping you waiting.' He

crossed to the floor-to-ceiling plate-glass window, turned his back on the magnificent harbour view, and thrust one hand into his trouser pocket.

Her expression was coolly aloof, although her eyes held the darkness of anger. 'Really? I imagine keeping me waiting is part of the game-play.'

Sassy, he mused, and mad. It made a change from simpering companions who held a diploma in superficial artificiality.

'If you had telephoned, my secretary could have arranged a suitable time,' Diego inferred mildly.

'Next week?' she parried with deliberate facetiousness, and incurred a cynical smile.

'The very reason I suggested we share dinner.'

'I have no desire to share anything with you.' She paused, then drew in a deep breath. 'Let's get down to business, shall we?' She indicated the sheaf of papers tabled together in a thick folder. 'I have the requisite proof, and a copy of your offer. Everything appears to be in order.'

'You sound surprised.'

Cassandra swept him a dark glance. 'I doubt there's anything you could do that would surprise me.'

'I imagine Cameron has relayed the deal is subject to a condition?'

Her eyes glittered with barely repressed anger. 'He said it was personal. *How* personal?'

'Two separate nights and one weekend with you.'

She felt as if some elusive force had picked her

up and flung her against the nearest wall. 'That's barbaric,' she managed at last.

'Call it what you will.'

It took her a few seconds to find her voice. 'Why?'

'Because it amuses me?'

Was this payback? For all the invitations he'd offered and she'd refused…because she could. Now, her refusal would have far-reaching implications. Did she have the strength of will to ruin her father, the firm he'd spent his life taking from strength to strength?

'An investment of twenty-three million dollars against all sage advice, allows for—' he paused deliberately '—a bonus, wouldn't you say?'

She didn't think, or pause to consider the consequences of her actions. She simply picked up the nearest thing to hand and threw it at him. The fact he fielded it neatly and replaced it down onto his desk merely infuriated her further.

'Who do you think you are?' Her voice was low, and held a quality even she didn't recognise.

Stupid question, she dismissed. He knew precisely who he was, what he wanted, and how to get it.

'I'd advise you to think carefully before you consider another foolish move,' Diego cautioned silkily.

Her eyes sparked brilliant blue fire. 'What did you expect?' Her voice rose a fraction. 'For me to fall into your arms expressing my undying gratitude?'

She didn't see the humour lurking in those dark

depths. If she had, she'd probably throw something else at him.

'I imagined a token resistance.'

Oh, he did, did he? 'You realise I could lay charges against you for coercion?'

'You could try.'

'Only to have your team of lawyers counter with misinterpretation, whereupon you withdraw your financial rescue package?'

'Yes.'

'Emotional blackmail is a detestable ploy.'

'It's a negotiable tool,' Diego corrected, and in that moment she hated him more than she thought it possible to hate anyone.

'No.' Dear God, had she actually said the verbal negation?

'No, you don't agree it's a negotiable tool?'

'I won't have sex with you.'

'You're not in any position to bargain.'

'I'm not for sale,' Cassandra evinced with dignity.

'Everything has its price.'

'That's your credo in life?'

He waited a beat. 'Do you doubt it?'

She'd had enough. 'We're about done, don't you think?' She tried for calm, and didn't quite make it as she hitched the strap of her shoulder bag as she turned towards the door.

Damn Cameron. Damn the whole sorry mess.

'There's just one more thing.'

She registered Diego's silky drawl, recognised the

underlying threat, and paused, turning to look at him.

'Cameron's homosexuality.'

Two words. Yet they had the power to stop the breath in her throat.

Diego del Santo couldn't possibly know. No one knew. At least, only Cameron, his partner, and herself.

Anxiety meshed with panic at the thought her father might catch so much as a whisper...

Dear God, *no.*

Alexander Preston-Villers might find it difficult to accept Cameron had steadily sent Preston-Villers to the financial wall. But he'd never condone or forgive his son's sexual proclivity.

An appalling sense of anguish permeated her bones, her soul. Who had Diego del Santo employed to discover something she imagined so well-hidden, it was virtually impossible to uncover?

How deep had he dug?

No stone unturned. The axiom echoed and re-echoed inside her brain.

It said much of the man standing before her, the lengths he was prepared to go to to achieve his objective.

'I hate you.' The words fell from her lips in a voice shaky with anger. She felt cold, so cold she was willing to swear her blood had turned to ice in her veins.

Diego inclined his head, his eyes darkly still as

he observed her pale features, the starkness of defeat clearly evident in her expression. 'At this moment, I believe you do.'

He'd won. They both knew it. There was only one thing she could hope for…his silence.

'Yes.' His voice was quiet. 'You have my word.'

'For which I should be grateful?' she queried bitterly.

He didn't answer. Instead, he indicated the chair she'd previously occupied. 'Why don't you sit down?'

He crossed to the credenza, extracted a glass, filled it with iced water from the bar fridge, then placed the glass in her hand.

Cassandra didn't want to sit. She preferred to be on her feet, poised for flight.

Diego moved towards his desk and leaned one hip against its edge. 'Shall we begin again?'

Dear heaven, how did she get through this? With as much dignity as possible, an inner voice prompted.

'The ball's in your court.'

Did she have any idea how vulnerable she looked? The slightly haunted quality evident in those stunning blue eyes, the translucence of her skin.

He remembered the taste of her, her fragrance, the soft, tentative response… He'd sought to imprint her with his touch, unclear of his motivation. A desire to shock, to punish? A lesson to be wary of men whose prime need was sex?

Instead, it had been she who'd left a lingering memory, unexpectedly stirring his soul…as well as another pertinent part of his anatomy. A pubescent temptress, unaware of her feminine power, he mused, wondering at the time how she'd react if he took advantage of her youth.

Sixteen-year-old girls were out of bounds. Especially when this particular sixteen-year-old was the cherished daughter of one of the city's industrial scions. Her brother, the elder by two years, should have known better than to bring her to a party where drinks were spiked and drugs were in plentiful supply. A fact he'd cursorily relayed before bundling brother and sister out of the host's house, then following in their wake.

Relationships, he'd had a few. Women he'd enjoyed, taking what was so willingly offered without much thought to permanence. As to commitment…there hadn't been any woman he'd wanted to make his own, exclusively. Happy-ever-after was a fallacy. Undying love, a myth.

For the past year one woman had teased his senses, yet she'd held herself aloof from every attempt he made to date her, and he'd had to content himself with a polite greeting whenever their social paths crossed.

Until now.

'As soon as our personal arrangement has satisfactorily concluded,' Diego drawled, 'I'll attach my signature to the relevant paperwork and organise for funds to be released.'

Cassandra registered his words, and felt her stomach contract in tangible pain. 'And when do you envisage our *personal arrangement* will begin?'

'Anyone would think you view sex with me as a penance.'

'Your ego must be enormous if you imagine I could possibly regard it as a pleasure.'

'Brave words,' Diego drawled, 'when you have no knowledge what manner of lover I am.'

The mere thought of that tall, muscular body engaged intimately with hers was enough to send heat spiralling from deep inside.

Instinct warned he was a practised lover, aware of all the pleasure pulses in a woman's body, and how to coax each and every one of them to vibrant life with the skilled touch of his mouth, his hands.

It was there, in the darkness of his gaze…the sensual confidence of a man well-versed in the desires of women.

A tiny shiver started at the base of her spine, and feathered its way to her nape, settled there, so she had to make a conscious effort to prevent it from appearing visible.

'Wednesday evening I'm attending a dinner party. I'll collect you at six-thirty. Pack whatever you need for the night.'

The day after tomorrow?

An hysterical laugh rose and died in her throat. So soon? Oh, God, why not? At least then the first night would be over. One down, one and a weekend to go.

'The remaining nights?' Dear heaven, how could she sound so calm?

'Saturday.'

She felt as if she were dying. 'And the last?'

'The following weekend.' His gaze never left hers. 'One million dollars will be deposited into the Preston-Villers business account following each of the three occasions you spend with me. Monday week, Preston-Villers' creditors will be paid off.'

'A *condition*, tenuously alluded to in the documentation as "being met to Diego del Santo's satisfaction", doesn't even begin to offer me any protection. What guarantee do I have you won't declare the offer documented as null and void on the grounds the *condition* hasn't been met to your satisfaction?'

'My word.'

She had to force her voice to remain steady, otherwise it would betray her by shattering into a hundred pieces. 'Sorry, but that won't cut it.'

'Do you know how close you walk to the edge of my tolerance?'

'Don't insult my intelligence by detailing a *condition* that has so many holes in it, even Blind Freddie could see through them!'

'You don't trust me?'

'No.'

He could walk away from the deal. It was what he *should* do. Twenty-three million dollars was no small amount of money, even if in the scheme of things it represented only a very small percentage of his investments.

He enjoyed the adrenalin charge in taking a worn-down company, injecting the necessary funds and making it work again.

'What is it you want?'

It was no time to lose her bravado. 'Something in writing detailing those nights, each comprising no more than twelve hours spent in your company, represents my sexual obligation to you, as covered by the term *condition*, and said obligation shall not be judged by my sexual performance.' She took a deep breath, and released it slowly. 'The original copy will be destroyed when you release funds in full into the Preston-Villers business account.'

She watched as he set up a laptop, keyed in data, activated the printer, proofread the printed copy, then attached his signature and handed her the page.

Cassandra read it, then she neatly folded the page and thrust it into her shoulder bag. Un-notarised, it wouldn't have much value in a court of law. But it was better than nothing.

The melodic burr of his cellphone provided the impetus she needed to escape.

Diego spared a glance at the illuminated dial, and cut the call. He moved to the door, opened it, then he led the way out to the main foyer and summoned the lift.

'Six-thirty, Wednesday evening,' he reminded as the electronic doors slid open.

It nearly killed her to act with apparent unconcern, when inside she was a quivering mess. 'I won't say it's been a pleasure,' Cassandra managed coolly as she depressed the appropriate button to take her down to ground level.

As a parting shot it lacked the impact she would have liked, but she took a degree of satisfaction in having the last word.

Two weeks from now she would have fulfilled Diego del Santo's *condition*.

Three, no, four nights in his bed. She could do it...couldn't she, and emerge emotionally unscathed?

CHAPTER THREE

Two evenings later Cassandra stood sipping excellent champagne in the lounge of a stunning Rose Bay mansion.

Guests mingled, some of whom she knew, and the conversation flowed. However, the evening, the venue, the fellow guests…none had as much impact on her as the man at her side.

Diego del Santo exuded practised charm, solicitous interest, and far too much sexual chemistry for any woman's peace of mind. Especially hers.

Worse, she was all too aware of the way her nervous tension escalated by the minute.

She didn't want to be here. More particularly, she didn't want to be linked to Diego del Santo in any way.

Yet she was bound to him, caught in an invisible trap, and the clock was ticking down towards the moment they were alone.

Even the thought of that large, lithe frame, naked, was enough to send her heartbeat into overdrive.

'More champagne?'

His voice was an inflected drawl as he indicated her empty flute, and he was close, too close for comfort, for she was supremely conscious of him, his fine tailoring, the exclusive cologne, and the man beneath the sophisticated exterior.

'No,' she managed politely. 'Thank you.' There was some merit in having one drink too many in order to endure the night. However, the evening was young, dinner would soon be served, and she valued her social reputation too much as well as her self-esteem to pass the next few hours in an alcoholic haze.

Choosing what to wear had seen her selecting one outfit after another and discarding most. In the end she'd opted for a bias-cut red silk dress with a soft, draped neckline and ribbon straps. Subtle make-up with emphasis on her eyes, and she'd swept her hair into a careless knot atop her head. Jewellery was an intricately linked neck chain with matching ear-studs.

Packing an overnight bag had been simple…she'd simply tossed in a change of clothes and a few necessities. A bag Diego had retrieved from her hand as she emerged from the foyer and deposited in the trunk of his car.

Quite what she expected she wasn't sure. There had been nothing overt in his greeting, and he made no attempt to touch her as he saw her seated in his stylish Aston Martin.

During the brief drive to their hosts' home he'd

kept conversation to a minimum…presumably influenced by her monosyllabic replies.

What did he expect? For her to smile and laugh? Act as if this was a *date*, for heaven's sake?

He'd made her part of a deal, and she hated him for it. Almost as much as she hated being thrust among a coterie of guests for several hours.

Guests who were undoubtedly curious at Diego's choice of partner for the evening. Or should that be curiosity at *her* choice of partner?

Had whispers of Preston-Villers' financial straits begun to circulate? And if they had, what context was placed on Cassandra Preston-Villers appearing at Diego's side? Would gossip allude the amalgamation had moved from the boardroom to the bedroom?

Cassandra told herself she didn't care…and knew she lied.

Dinner. Dear heaven, how could she *eat*? Her stomach felt as if it were tied in knots, and primed to reject any food she sent its way.

'Relax.'

Diego's voice was a quiet drawl as they took their seats at the elegantly set table, and she offered a stunning smile. 'I'm perfectly relaxed.'

There were numerous courses, each a perfect complement served with the artistry and flair of a professional chef.

Compliments were accorded, and Cassandra

added her own, painfully aware her tastebuds had gone on strike.

She conversed with fellow guests, almost on autopilot, playing the social game with the ease of long practice. Although afterwards she held little recollection of any discussion.

Diego was *there*, a constant entity, and the build-up of tension accelerated as the evening progressed. The light brush of his hand on hers succeeded in sending her pulse into overdrive, and she almost forgot to breathe when he leaned close to refill her water glass.

She began to pray for the evening to end, to be free from the constraints of polite society. At least when they were alone she could discard the façade and fence verbal swords with him!

Somehow she made it through the seemingly endless meal, and it was a relief to retreat to the lounge to linger over coffee.

Diego seemed in no hurry to leave, and it was almost eleven when he indicated they bid their hosts goodnight.

The short drive to nearby suburban Point Piper was achieved in silence, and Cassandra felt her body stiffen as he activated the electronic gates guarding the entrance to a curved driveway illuminated by strategically placed lights leading to a large home whose architecturally designed exterior and interior had featured in one of the glossy magazines soon after its completion.

The Aston Martin eased beneath electronic garage doors and slid to a halt as the doors closed behind them with an imperceptible click.

Trapped.

Take me home. The words rose as a silent cry, only to die unuttered in her throat.

You have to go through with this, a silent voice prompted pitilessly. Think of Alexander, Cameron.

But what about *me*?

Diego popped the trunk, then emerged from behind the wheel and retrieved her bag as she slipped out of the passenger seat.

In silence she preceded him indoors, then walked at his side as he moved into the main foyer.

With a sense of increasing desperation she focused on the generous dimensions, the gently curving staircase with its intricately designed balustrade leading to the upper floor. A crystal chandelier hung suspended from the high ceiling, and solid mahogany cabinets added to the Spanish influence. Art graced the walls, providing an ambience of wealth.

Had he personally chosen all this, or consulted with an interior decorator?

Diego deposited her bag at the foot of the staircase, then he indicated a door on his right. 'A nightcap?'

Cassandra watched as he crossed the foyer and

revealed a spacious lounge. The thought of exchanging polite conversation and playing *pretend* was almost more than she could bear.

The entire evening had been a preliminary to the moment she'd need to share his bed. Drawing it out any further seemed pointless.

'If you don't mind, I'd prefer to get on with it.'

She was nervous. He could sense it in her voice, see the way her pulse jumped at the base of her throat, and he took pleasure from it.

'Cut to the chase?'

His query was a silky drawl that sent an icy feather sliding down her spine. 'Yes.'

Diego gave an imperceptible shrug as he closed the door and indicated the staircase. 'By all means.'

Was she *mad*? Oh, for heaven's sake, she chided silently. He's only a man, like any other.

They'd have sex, she'd sleep, he'd wake her at dawn for more sex, then she'd shower, dress, and get a cab to work.

How big a deal could it be?

The way the blood fizzed through her veins, heating her body was incidental. The rapid thudding of her heart was merely due to nervous tension. Stress, anxiety…take your pick. A direct result of the sexual price she'd agreed to pay with a man she told herself she didn't like.

Together they ascended the curved staircase, then

turned left, traversing the balustraded gallery to a lavishly furnished master suite.

Cassandra entered the room, only to falter to a halt as uncertainty froze her limbs. *Think,* she silently cajoled. Slip off your stiletto-heeled pumps, remove your jewellery…

The ear-studs were easy, but her fingers shook as she reached for the clasp at her nape.

'Let me do that,' Diego said quietly, and moved in close.

Far too close. She could sense him behind her, almost *feel* the touch of that powerful body against her own. How much space separated them? An inch? If she leant back, her shoulders would brush his chest.

Oh, hell, *should* she, and make it easy for herself? Play the seductress and melt into his arms?

His fingers touched her nape and she unconsciously held her breath as he dealt with the clasp. Then it was done, and she took a step away from him as he dropped the jewellery into her hand.

Cassandra crossed to where Diego had placed her bag and tucked the jewellery into a pouch. When she turned he was close, and her stomach clenched as he reached for the pins in her hair.

His fingers grazed the graceful curve of her neck, and sensation shivered the length of her spine.

'Beautiful.'

His silky murmur did strange things to her equilibrium, and she fought against the almost mesmeric fascination threatening to undermine her defences.

It would be so easy to sway towards him, angle her head, fasten her mouth on his and simply sink in.

Yet to meekly comply meant she condoned his actions, and there wasn't a hope in hell she'd ever forgive his manipulation.

'Let's not pretend this is anything other than what it is.'

Cassandra reached for the zip fastener on her dress, and managed to slide it down a few inches before his hand halted its progress.

'Highly priced sex?' Diego queried in a faintly accented drawl.

'You got it in one.'

She was nervous, and that intrigued him. Any other woman would have played the coquette, and provocatively stripped for his pleasure. Teasing, before undressing *him*, then moving in to begin a practised seduction before he took control.

'If you want to unwrap the package…' Cassandra managed what she hoped was a negligent shrug '…then go ahead.'

Diego's eyes narrowed, and his voice was a husky drawl. 'How could a man resist the temptation?'

He slid the zip fastener all the way down, then lifted his hands to the shoestring straps, slipping them over each shoulder so the gown slithered to a heap on the carpeted floor.

The only garment that saved her from total nudity was a silk thong brief, and she forced herself to stand still beneath his studied appraisal.

Her eyes blazed blue fire as his gaze lingered on her breasts, skimmed low, then lifted to meet the defiant outrage apparent.

With slow, deliberate movements he removed his shoes and socks, shed his jacket, loosened his tie and removed it, then he freed his trousers before tending to the buttons on his shirt.

He was something else. Broad shoulders, lean hips, a washboard stomach, olive-toned skin sheathed an enviable abundance of hardened sinew and muscle. Fit, not pumped, with a sleekness that denoted undeniable strength.

Black silk briefs did little to hide his arousal, and she hated the warm tinge that coloured her cheeks as he swept back the bedcovers.

With unhurried steps he closed the distance between them, and her eyes widened fractionally as he touched a gentle finger to her lips and traced the lower curve. Warmth flooded her body and became pulsing heat as he cupped her face, and a soundless groan rose and died in her throat as he lowered his head down to hers.

Whatever she'd expected, it wasn't the slow, evocative touch of his mouth on her own, or the way his tongue slid between her lips as his hands cupped her face.

She felt his thumbs brush each cheek, and the breath caught in her throat as he angled his mouth and went in deep.

He tugged at her senses and tore them to shreds, destroying the protective barrier she'd built up against him.

Her hands lifted to his shoulders in a bid to hang on, only to rest briefly, hesitantly there as he slid a hand to capture her nape while the other skimmed the length of her spine to curve over her bottom and pull her close.

In one fluid movement he dispensed with the scrap of silk, and she gasped as he sought the warm heat at the apex of her thighs.

There was little she could do to prevent his skilled fingers wreaking havoc there. He knew where to touch and how…light strokes that almost drove her wild, and just when she thought she couldn't stand any more he eased off, only to have her gasp as the oral stimulation intensified to another level.

'Let go,' Diego instructed huskily, and absorbed her despairing groan.

Her body might be tempted, but her mind wasn't in sync. Had it ever been? she registered cynically, aware that for her intimacy, while pleasurable, was hardly a mind-blowing experience. Why should it be any different this time?

Fake it, a silent imp prompted. Just…get it over with, then it'll be done. For tonight.

His hands shifted to cup her face. 'Don't.'

Cassandra stilled at his softly voiced admonition, and cast him a startled glance. 'I don't know what you mean.'

He traced the lower curve of her mouth with the pad of his thumb, and saw her eyes flare. 'Yes, you do.'

She could feel the warmth colour her cheeks. What was it with this man that he could lay bare her secrets?

Her previous partners had been so consumed with their own pleasure they hadn't cared about her own.

A strangled laugh rose and died in her throat. It wasn't as if she'd had numerous partners…only two, each of whom had declared undying devotion while fixing an eye on her father's wealth.

'I don't want to be here with you.'

'Perhaps not.' He waited a beat. 'Yet.'

'Are you sure there's enough space in this room for both you and your ego?'

His husky laugh was almost her undoing. 'You doubt I can make you want me?'

'It would be a first.' The words were out before she thought to stop them, and she saw his eyes narrow.

He was silent for what seemed an age, then he released her. In one fluid movement he reached for the bedcovers, restored them to their former position, then he indicated the bed. 'Get in.'

Uncertainty momentarily showed in her features.

'You prefer the bed?'

'It's more comfortable.'

Comfort. It beat tumbling to the carpeted floor. Although somehow she doubted Diego was prone to awkward moves.

'To sleep,' Diego added, watching confusion cloud her eyes.

'Sleep?' She felt as if she was repeating everything he said.

His gaze speared hers. 'For now,' he qualified evenly. 'Does that bother you?'

A stay of execution? She wasn't sure whether to be pleased or peeved. 'A reprieve? Should I thank you?'

'Don't push it, *querida*.' His voice held the softness of silk, but the warning was pure steel.

Capitulation would be a wise choice, she perceived, and crossed to her bag, extracted a large cotton T-shirt and pulled it on, then after a moment's hesitation she joined him in the large bed, settling as far away from him as possible.

Diego pressed a remote module and doused the lights, and Cassandra felt her body tense in the darkness as she waited for the moment he might reach for her.

Except he didn't, and she lay still, aware of the moment his breathing slowed to a steady pace.

Dammit, he was asleep! As easily and quickly as that, he'd been able to relax sufficiently to sleep.

Leaving her to lie awake to seethe in silence. The temptation to fist her hand and *punch* him was paramount! How dared he simply switch off? How *could* he?

She still had the imprint of his hands on her body, and her mouth felt slightly swollen from the touch of his.

Unfulfilled anticipation. Dear heaven, she couldn't be disappointed, surely?

Diego del Santo was someone she intensely disliked, *hated,* she amended. Just because there was an exigent chemistry between them didn't alter a thing.

How could she *sleep*, for heaven's sake? He was *there*, his large, powerfully muscled body within touching distance.

Was it imagination, or could she feel his warmth? Sense the heat of his sex, even in repose?

It was madness. Insane. She closed her eyes and summoned sleep, only to stifle the groan that rose and died in her throat.

Her limbs, her whole body seemed stiff, and she'd have given anything to roll over and punch her pillow, then resettle into a more comfortable position.

Yet if she moved, she might disturb Diego, and that wasn't a favoured option.

Cassandra counted sheep…to no avail. She concentrated on an intricate jewellery design she was working on, visualised the finished item and made a few minor adjustments.

How long had she been lying in the dark? Ten, twenty minutes? Thirty? How long until the dawn? Four, five hours?

There was a faint movement, then the room was bathed in soft light, and Diego loomed close, his upper body supported on one elbow.

'Can't sleep?' His voice was a husky drawl that curled round her nerve-ends and tugged a little.

Her eyes were large, and far too dark, her features pale.

'I didn't know you were awake.' He must sleep like a cat, attuned to the slightest movement, the faintest sound.

'Headache?'

It would be so easy to acquiesce, but she wasn't into fabrication. 'No.'

He lifted a hand and trailed gentle fingers across her cheek. 'Waging an inner battle?'

There was nothing like the witching midnight hour to heighten vulnerability. 'Yes.'

His mouth curved into a musing smile. 'Honesty is a quality so rarely found in women.'

'You obviously haven't met the right woman.'

Was that her voice? It sounded impossibly husky. *Sexy,* she amended, slightly shocked, and flinched as his fingers traced a path to her temple and tucked a swathe of hair behind her ear.

There was a sense of unreality in the conversation. She was conscious of the room, the bed...then the man, only the man became her total focus.

The pad of his thumb traced her lower lip, depressed its centre, then slid to her chin, holding it fast as he fastened his mouth on hers, coaxing in a prelude to the deliberate seduction of her senses.

The subtle exploration became an evocative sensual possession that took hold of her inhibitions and dispensed with them...far too easily for her peace of mind.

She should withdraw and retreat, protest a little. Except his touch held a magic she couldn't resist, and she groaned as his hands caressed her breasts, shaped the sensitive flesh, then tantalised the burgeoning peaks.

Heat flooded her veins, filling her body with sensual warmth as she arched against the path of his hand, and he absorbed her soft cry as he caught hold of her T-shirt and tugged it free.

For several long seconds she bore his silent appraisal, glimpsed the vital, almost electric energy apparent, and knew instinctively that intimacy would surely take place.

The intention, the driven need was there, clearly

evident, and sensation spiralled through her body at the thought of his possession.

All her skin-cells came achingly alive, acutely sensitive to his touch as he lowered his head over her breast and suckled its tender peak. Then she cried out as he used his teeth to take her to the brink between pain and pleasure.

Cassandra slid her fingers through his hair and tugged, willing him to cease, only to gasp as he trailed a path to her waist, paused to circle her navel with his tongue before edging slowly towards the apex of her thighs.

He couldn't, wouldn't...surely?

But he did, with brazen disregard for her plea to desist. The level of intimacy shocked her, and she fought against the skilled stroking, the heat and thrust of his tongue as he sent her high. So high, the acute sensory spiral tore a startled cry from her throat.

Just as she thought the sensation couldn't become more intense, it came again, so acutely piercing it arrowed through her body, an all-consuming flame soaring from deep within.

Dear heaven. The fervent whisper fell from her lips as an irreverent prayer as Diego shifted slightly and trailed his lips over her sensitised flesh to possess her mouth in a kiss that took her deep, so deep she simply gave herself over to it and shared the sensual feast.

Somewhere in the deep recesses of her mind an alarm bell sounded, and she stilled. 'Protection?'

'Taken care of.'

Cassandra felt him nudge her thighs apart, the probe of his arousal as he eased into her, and her shocked gasp at his size died in her throat.

His slick heat magnetised her, and she felt her muscles tense around him, then relax in a rhythm that gradually accepted his length. He stilled, his mouth a persuasive instrument as he plundered at will, sweeping her high until all rational thought vanished.

Then he began to move, slowly at first, so slowly she felt the passage inch by inch, and just as she began to think he intended to disengage, he slid in to the hilt in one excruciatingly sensual thrust, repeating the movement as he increased the pace. Until the rhythm became an hypnotic entity she had no power to resist.

Mesmeric, urgent, libidinous…it became something she'd never experienced before. An intoxicating captivation of her senses as he swept them high to a point of magical ecstasy.

She had no memory of the scream torn from her throat, the way her nails raked his ribs, or how she sought his flesh with her teeth. She was a wild wanton, driven beyond mere desire to a primitive place where passion became an incandescent entity.

Diego brought her down slowly, gently, soothing her quivering body until she stilled in his arms.

There were tears trickling down each cheek, and he felt his heart constrict at her vulnerability.

She felt exposed. As if this man had somehow managed to see into her heart, her soul, and that everything she was, all her secrets were laid bare.

There was little she could gain from his expression, and her mouth shook as he carefully rolled onto his back, taking her with him.

His gaze held hers in the soft light, and she couldn't look away. There were no words, nothing she could say, and the breath hitched in her throat as he lifted both hands to her breasts.

With the utmost care he tested their weight, then traced the gentle swell, using his thumb pad to caress the swollen peaks.

Her skin felt sensitive to his touch as he cupped her waist, then slid to her hips.

Cassandra felt her eyes widen as he began to swell inside her, and a soundless gasp parted her lips as he began a slow, undulating movement.

Again? He was ready for more?

She caught the rhythm and matched it, enjoying the dominant position, and what followed became the ride of her life…and his, for there was no doubting his passion, or the moment of his climax as it joined with her own.

Afterwards he drew her down against him and

cradled her close until her breathing, his own, returned to normal.

She could have slept right there, her cheek cushioned against his chest, and she began to protest as
he disengaged and eased her to lie beside him.

Then she did voice a protest as he slid from the
bed and swept her into his arms.

'What are you doing?' Her faintly scandalised
query held an edge of panic as he crossed to the *en
suite* and entered the spacious shower cubicle.

'We can't share a shower,' Cassandra protested,
and earned a husky laugh.

'We just shared the ultimate in intimacy,' Diego
drawled as he picked up the soap and began smoothing it over her skin.

So they had, but this…this was something else,
and she put a hand to his chest in silent remon-
strance.

'No.'

He didn't stop. 'Afterwards we sleep.'

She pushed him. Or at least she tried, but he was
an immovable force. 'I can take care of myself.'

'Indulge me.'

'Diego—'

'I like the sound of my name on your lips.'

'Please!' His touch was a little too up close and
personal, and he was invading her private space in
a way no man had done before.

'You get to have your turn any minute soon,' he

drawled with amusement, then had the audacity to chuckle as she took a well-aimed swipe at his shoulder.

'If you want to play, *querida*, I'm only too willing to oblige.'

'I'm all played out.' It was the truth, for exhaustion was beginning to overpower her, combined with the soporific spray of hot water, heated steam and lateness of the hour. Plus she hurt in places she'd never hurt before.

He finished her ablutions, then set about completing his own. Within minutes he turned off the water, snagged a bath towel and towelled her dry before applying the towel to his own torso.

Seconds later he led her into the bedroom and pulled her down onto the bed, settled the covers, then doused the light.

With one fluid movement her gathered her in against him and held her there, aware of the moment tiredness overcame her reluctance and she slept.

CHAPTER FOUR

CASSANDRA woke slowly, aware within seconds this wasn't her bed, her room, or her apartment. Realisation dawned, and she turned her head cautiously…only to see she was the sole occupant of the large bed.

Of Diego there was no sign, and she checked the time, gasped in exasperated dismay, then she slid to her feet, gathered fresh underwear and day clothes from her bag and made for the *en suite*.

Fifteen minutes later she gathered up her bag and moved down to the lower floor. She could smell fresh coffee, toast…and felt her stomach rumble in growling protest as she made her way towards the kitchen.

Diego stood at the servery, dressed in dark trousers, a business shirt unbuttoned at the neck, and a matching dark jacket rested over the back of a chair with a tie carelessly tossed on top of it.

He looked far too alive for a man who'd spent the greater part of the night engaged in physical activity, and just the sight of him was enough to shred her nerves.

'I was going to give you another five minutes,'

he drawled. 'Then come fetch you.' He indicated the carafe. 'Coffee?'

'Please.' She felt awkward, and incredibly vulnerable. 'Then I'll call a cab.'

Diego extracted a plate of eggs and toast from a warming tray. 'I'll drive you home. Sit down and eat.'

'I'm not hungry.'

He subjected her to a raking appraisal, saw the darkened shadows beneath her eyes, the faint edge of tiredness. 'Eat,' he insisted. 'Then we'll leave.'

Any further protest would be fruitless, and besides, the eggs looked good. She took a seat and did justice to the food, sipped the strong, hot black coffee, and felt more ready to face the day.

As soon as she finished he pulled on his tie and adjusted it, then shrugged into his jacket.

She began clearing the table with the intention of doing the dishes.

'Leave them.'

'It'll only take a few minutes.'

'I have a cleaning lady. Leave them.'

Without a word she picked up her bag and followed him through to the garage.

The distance between Point Piper and Double Bay amounted to a few kilometres, and Cassandra slid open the door within seconds of Diego drawing the car to a halt outside the entrance of her apartment building.

There wasn't an adequate word that came to

mind, and she didn't offer one as she walked away from him.

The cat gave an indignant miaow as she unlocked her door, and she dropped her bag, put down fresh food, then took the lift down to the basement car park.

Minutes later she eased her vintage Porsche onto the road and battled morning peak-hour traffic to reach her place of work.

Concentration on the job in hand proved difficult as she attempted to dispel Diego's powerful image.

Far too often she was reminded of his possession. Dear heaven, she could still *feel* him. Tender internal tissues provided a telling evidence, and just the thought of her reaction to their shared intimacy was enough to bring her to the point of climax.

As if last night wasn't enough, he'd reached for her in the early dawn hours, employing what she reflected was considerable stealth to arouse her before she was fully awake and therefore conscious of his intention.

Worse, he had stilled any protest she might have voiced with a skilled touch, inflaming her senses and attacking the fragile tenure of her control.

How could she react with such electrifying passion to a man she professed to hate? To transcend the physical and unleash myriad emotions to become a willing wanton in his arms. Accepting a degree of intimacy she'd never imagined being sufficiently comfortable with to condone.

Yet she had. Swept away beyond reason or rational thought by sexual chemistry at its zenith.

Her cellphone buzzed, signalling an incoming text message, and she checked it during her lunch break, then responded by keying in Cameron's number.

'Just checking in,' her brother reassured.

'Enquiring how I survived Act One of the three-act night play?'

'Cynicism, Cassandra?'

'I'm entitled, don't you think?'

'Act Two takes place…when?'

'Saturday night.'

'I appreciate—'

'Don't,' she said fiercely, 'go there.' She cut the connection, automatically reached for the Caesar salad she'd ordered, only to take one mouthful and push the plate aside. Instead, she ate the accompanying Turkish bread and sipped the latte before returning to the workshop.

Mid-afternoon she gave in to a throbbing headache and took a painkiller to ease it, then she fixed the binocular microscope, adjusted the light, and set to work.

Cassandra was relieved when the day came to an end, and she stopped off at a supermarket *en route* to her apartment and collected groceries, cat food and fresh fruit.

Essential provisions, she mused as she carried the sack indoors, unpacked it, then she fed the cat, prepared fish and salad for herself. Television interested her for an hour, then she opened her laptop, double-checked design measurements and made some minor adjustments, then she closed everything down and went to bed.

Within minutes she felt the familiar pad of the cat's tread as it joined her and settled against her legs. Companionship and unconditional love, she mused with affection as she sought solace in sleep.

Difficult, when the one man she resented invaded her thoughts, filling her mind, and invaded her dreams.

Diego del Santo had a lot to answer for, Cassandra swore as the next day proved no less stressful. Her stomach executed a downward dive every time her cellphone rang as she waited for him to confirm arrangements for Saturday night.

By Friday evening she was a bundle of nerves, cursing him volubly…which did no good at all and startled the cat.

Consequently when she picked up the phone Saturday morning and heard his voice, it was all she could do to remain civil.

'I'll collect you at six-thirty. Dinner first, then we're due to attend a gallery exhibition.'

'If you'll advise an approximate time you expect to return home,' Cassandra managed stiffly, 'I'll meet you there.'

'No.'

Her fingers tightened on the cellphone casing. 'What do you mean…*no*?' She felt the anger begin a slow simmer, and took a deep breath to control it. 'You can take someone else to dinner and the gallery.'

'Go from one woman to another?'

He sounded amused, damn him. 'Socialising with you doesn't form part of the arrangement.'

'It does, however, entitle me to twelve hours of your time on two of our three legally binding occasions. If you'd prefer not to socialise, I'm more than willing to have you spend those twelve hours in my bed.'

She wanted to kill him. At the very least, she'd do him an injury. 'Minimising sex with you is my main priority.' Trying to remain calm took considerable effort. 'As I'll need my car for the morning, I'll drive to your place.'

'Six-thirty, Cassandra.' He cut the connection before she could say another word.

Choosing what to wear didn't pose a problem, for she led a reasonably active social life and possessed the wardrobe to support it.

For a brief moment she considered something entirely inappropriate, only to dismiss it and go with *stunning*.

Soft and feminine was the *in* style, and she had just the gown in jade silk georgette. Spaghetti straps, a deep V-neckline, and a handkerchief hemline. Guaranteed *wow* factor, she perceived as she swept her hair into a careless knot and added the finishing touches to her make-up.

It was six-twenty-five when she drew her car to a halt outside the gates guarding the entrance to Diego's home. Almost on cue they were electronically released, and she wondered whether it was by advance courtesy on his part or due to a sophisticated alarm system.

The Aston Martin was parked outside the main entrance, and Diego opened the front door as she slid out from her car.

Cassandra inclined her head in silent greeting and crossed to the Aston Martin.

'A punctual woman,' Diego drawled, and incurred a piercing glance.

'You said six-thirty.' She subjected him to a deliberate appraisal, taking in the dark dinner suit, the crisp white shirt, black bow-tie…and endeavoured to control the sudden leap of her pulse. 'Shall we leave?'

Polite, cool. She could do both. For now.

'No overnight bag?'

'I'll get it.' She did, and he placed it indoors before tending to the alarm.

'You've dressed to impress,' Diego complimented, subjecting her to a raking appraisal that had male appreciation at its base, and something else she didn't care to define.

There was an edge of mockery apparent, and she offered a practised smile. 'That should be…to *kill*,' she amended as he unlocked the car door, saw her seated, then crossed round the front to slide in behind the wheel.

'Should I be on guard for hidden weapons?'

Cassandra shot him a considering glance. 'Not my style.'

'But making a fashion statement is?'

'It's a woman's prerogative,' she responded with a certain wryness. 'Armour for all the visual feminine daggers that'll be aimed at my back tonight.'

'In deference to my so-called reputation?'

'Got it in one.'

The sound of his husky laughter became lost as he ignited the engine, and she remained silent for the relatively short drive to Double Bay, electing to attempt civility as the *maître d'* seated them at a reserved table.

'Australia must appeal to you,' she broached in an attempt at conversation. 'You've been based in Sydney for the past year.'

They'd progressed through the starter and were waiting for the main.

Diego settled back in his chair and regarded her with thoughtful speculation. 'I have business interests in several countries.' He regarded her with musing indolence. 'And homes in many.'

'Therefore one assumes your time of residence here is fairly transitory.'

'Possibly.'

Cassandra picked up her wine glass and took an

appreciative sip. 'Hearsay accords you a devious past.'

'Do you believe that?'

She considered him carefully. 'Social rumour can be misleading.'

'Invariably.'

There was a hardness apparent, something dangerous, almost lethal lurking deep beneath the surface. He bore the look of a man who'd seen much, weathered more...and survived.

'I think you enjoy the mystery of purported supposition.' She waited a beat. 'And you're too streetwise to have skated over the edge of the law.'

'Gracias.' His voice held wry cynicism.

The waiter presented their main, topped up their wine glasses, then retreated.

Cassandra picked up her cutlery and speared a succulent morsel. 'Do you have family in New York?'

'A brother.' The sole survivor of a drive-by shooting that had killed both their parents. A shocking event that happened within months of his initial sojourn in Sydney, the reason he'd taken the next flight home...and stayed to build his fortune.

It was almost nine when they entered the gallery. Guests stood in segregated groups. The men deep in discussion on subjects which would vary from the state of the country's economy to the latest business acquisition, and whether the current wife was aware of the latest mistress.

The women, on the other hand, discussed the latest fashion showing, which cosmetic surgeon was currently in vogue, speculated who was conducting a clandestine affair, and what the husband would need to part with in order to soothe the wife and retain the mistress.

The names changed, Cassandra accorded wryly, but the topics remained the same.

Tonight's exhibition was more about being seen than the purchase of a sculpture or painting. Yet the evening would be a success, due to the fact only those with buying power and social status received invitations.

Should nothing appeal, it was considered *de rigueur* to donate a sizeable cheque to a nominated charity.

Uniformed waitresses were circulating proffering trays with canapés, while waiters offered champagne and orange juice.

'Feel free to mix and mingle.'

Their presence had been duly noted, their coupling providing speculation which would, Cassandra deduced, run rife.

Had news already spread about the financial state of Preston-Villers? It was too much to hope it would be kept under wraps for long.

'Let's take a look at the exhibits,' Diego suggested smoothly, and led her towards the nearest section of paintings.

Modern impressionists held little appeal, and she

found herself explaining why as they moved on to examine some metal sculptures, one of which appeared so bizarre it held her attention only from the viewpoint of discovering what it was supposed to represent.

'Diego. I didn't expect to see you here.'

The silky feminine purr held a faint accent, and Cassandra turned to see Alicia move close to Diego.

Much too close.

'Cassandra,' the model acknowledged. 'I haven't seen Cameron here tonight.'

A barbed indication she should get a life, a lover…and not resort to accompanying her brother to most social events? Cameron relied on her presence as a cover, while she was content to provide it. A comfort zone that suited them both. Two previous relationships hadn't encouraged her to have much faith in the male of the species. One man had regarded her as a free ride in life on her father's money; the other had wanted marriage in order to gain eventual chairmanship of Preston-Villers.

'Cameron was unable to attend,' she answered smoothly. It was a deviation from the truth, and one she had no intention of revealing.

Alicia looked incredible, buffed to perfection from the tip of her Italian-shod feet to the elegantly casual hairstyle. Gowned in black silk which clung to her curves in a manner which belied the use of underwear, she was a magnet for every man in the room.

Alicia's eyes narrowed fractionally as a fellow guest commandeered Diego's attention, drawing him into a discussion with two other men.

'You're here tonight with Diego?' The query held incredulous disbelief. 'Darling, isn't he a little out of your league?'

Cassandra kept her voice light. 'The implication being…?'

'He's rich, primitive, and dangerous.' Alicia spared her a sweeping glance. 'You'd never handle him.'

This was getting bitchy. 'And you can?'

The model cast her a sweeping glance, then uttered a deprecatory laugh. 'Oh, *please*, darling.'

Well, that certainly said it all!

She resisted the temptation to tell the model the joke was on her. *Handling* Diego was the last thing she wanted to do!

'In that case,' Cassandra managed sweetly, 'why did Diego invite me along when you're so—' she paused fractionally '—obviously available?'

Anger blazed briefly in those beautiful dark blue eyes, then assumed icy scorn. 'The novelty factor?'

If you only knew! 'You think so?' She manufactured a faint smile. 'Maybe he simply tired of having women fall over themselves to gain his attention.'

Alicia placed a hand on Cassandra's arm. 'Playing hard to get is an ill-advised game. You'll end up being hurt.'

'And you care?'

'Don't kid yourself, darling.'

'Are you done?' She offered a practised smile, and barely restrained an audible gasp as Alicia dug hard, lacquered fingernails into her arm.

'Oh, I think so. For now.'

Anything was better than fencing verbal swords with the glamour queen, and Cassandra began threading her way towards the remaining exhibits, pausing now and then to converse with a fellow guest.

There was a display of bronze sculptures, and one in particular caught her eye. It was smaller than the others, and lovingly crafted to portray an elderly couple seated together on a garden stool. The man's arm enclosed the woman's shoulders as she leaned into him. Their expressive features captured a look that touched her heart. Everlasting love.

'Quite something, isn't it?' a male voice queried at her side.

Cassandra turned and offered a smile. 'Yes,' she agreed simply.

'Gregor Stanislau.' He inclined his head. 'And you are?'

'Cassandra.'

His grin was infectious. 'You have an interest in bronze?' He indicated the remaining sculptures and led her past each of them. He was knowledgeable, explaining techniques, discussing what he perceived as indiscernible flaws detracting from what could have been perfection.

'The elderly couple seated on the stool. It's your work, isn't it?'

He spread his hands in an expressive gesture. 'Guilty.'

'It's beautiful,' she complimented. 'Is it the only piece you have displayed here?'

He inclined his head. 'The couple were modelled on my grandparents. It was to be a gift to them, but I was unable to complete it in time.'

She didn't need to ask. 'Would you consider selling it?'

'To you?' He named a price she considered exorbitant, and she shook her head.

He looked genuinely regretful. 'I'm reasonably negotiable. Make me an offer.'

'Forty per cent of your original figure, plus the gallery's commission,' Diego drawled from behind her, and she turned in surprise as he moved to her side. How long had he been standing there? She hadn't even sensed his presence.

Gregor looked severely offended. 'That's an outrage.'

Diego's smile was superficially pleasant, but the hardness apparent in his eyes was not. 'Would you prefer me to insist on a professional appraisal?'

'Seventy-five per cent, and I'll consider it sold.'

'The original offer stands.'

'Your loss.' The sculptor effected a negligible shrug and retreated among the guests.

'You had no need to negotiate on my behalf,'

Cassandra declared, annoyed at his intervention. 'I was more than capable of handling him.'

Diego shot her a mocking glance, which proved a further irritation. Did he think *blonde* and *naïve* automatically went hand-in-hand?

Wrong. 'He saw me admiring it, figured I was an easy mark, so he spun a sentimental tale with the aim to double his profit margin.' She lifted one eyebrow and deliberately allowed her mouth to curve in a winsome smile. 'How am I doing so far?'

His lips twitched a little. 'Just fine.'

Cassandra inclined her head. 'Thank you.'

'I can't wait to see your follow-up action.'

'Watch and learn.'

'At a guess,' he inclined indolently, 'you'll file a complaint with the gallery owner, who'll then offer to sell you the sculpture at a figure less than its purported value, as a conscience salve for the sculptor's misrepresentation.'

A slow smile curved her mouth, and her eyes sparkled with musing humour. 'You're good.'

Cassandra was discreet. No doubt it helped her father was a known patron of the arts, and the name Preston-Villers instantly recognisable. Apologies were forthcoming, she arranged payment and organised collection, then she turned to find Alicia deep in conversation with Diego.

Nothing prepared her for the momentary shaft of pain that shot through her body. It was ridiculous, and she hated her reaction almost as much as she hated *him*.

Diego del Santo was merely an aberration. A man who'd callously manipulated a set of circumstances to his personal advantage. So what if he was a highly skilled lover, sensitive to a woman's needs? There were other men equally as skilled... Men with blue-blood birth lines, educated in the finest private schools, graduating with honours from university to enter the fields of commerce, medicine, law.

She'd met them, socialised with them...and never found the spark to ignite her emotions. Until Diego.

It was insane.

Was Alicia his current companion? Certainly she'd seen them together at a few functions over the past month or so. There could be no doubt Alicia was hell-bent on digging her claws into him.

'Cassandra—*darling*. I was hoping to find you here. How *are* you?'

There were any number of society matrons in the city, but Annouska Pendelton presided at the top of their élite heap.

The air-kiss routine, the firm grasp of Annouska's manicured fingers on her own formed an integral part of the greeting process.

Annouska working the room, Cassandra accorded silently, very aware of the matron's charity work and the excessively large sums of money she managed to persuade the rich and famous to donate to the current worthy cause.

'How is dear Alexander?' There was a click of the tongue. 'So very sad his health is declining.' There was a second's pause. 'I see you're with Diego del Santo this evening. An interesting and influential man.'

'Yes,' Cassandra agreed sweetly. 'Isn't he?'

Annouska's gaze shifted. 'Ah, Diego.' Her smile held charm. 'We were just talking about you.'

He stood close, much too close. If she moved a fraction of an inch her arm would come into contact with him. The scent of his cologne teased her nostrils, subtle, expensive, and mingled with the clean smell of freshly laundered linen.

'Indeed?' His voice was a lazy honeyed drawl that sent all her fine body hairs on alert.

'You must both come to next month's soirée.' The matron relayed details with her customary unfailing enthusiasm. 'Invitations will be in the mail early in the week.' She pressed Cassandra's fingers, then transferred them to Diego's forearm. 'Enjoy the evening.'

'Would you like coffee?' Diego queried as Annouska moved on to her next quarry.

What I'd like is to go home to my own apartment and sleep in my own bed…alone. However, that wasn't going to happen.

Already her nerves were playing havoc at the thought of what the night would bring.

'No?' He took hold of her hand and threaded his fingers through her own. 'In that case we'll leave.'

She attempted to pull free from his grasp, and failed miserably. 'Alicia will be disappointed.'

'You expect me to qualify that?'

Cassandra didn't answer, and made another furtive effort to remove her hand. '*Must* you?'

It took several long minutes to ease their way towards the exit, and she caught Alicia's venomous glare as they left the gallery.

'Do you mind?' This time she dug her nails into the back of his hand. 'I'm not going to escape and run screaming onto the street.'

'You wouldn't get far.'

'I don't need to be reminded I owe you.'

The Aston Martin was parked adjacent to the gallery and only a short-distance walk. Yet he didn't release his grasp until he'd unlocked the car.

She didn't offer so much as a word during the drive to Point Piper, and she slid from the seat the instant Diego brought the car to a halt inside the garage.

It wasn't late by social standards, but she'd been in a state of nervous tension all day anticipating the evening and how it would end.

Dear heaven, she *knew* what to expect. There was even a part of her that *wanted* his possession. What woman wouldn't want to experience sensual heaven? she queried silently.

So why did she feel so angry? Diego del Santo wasn't hers. She had no tags on him whatsoever. He was free to date anyone, and Alicia Vandernoot was undoubtedly a tigress in bed.

Wasn't that what men wanted in a woman? A whore in the bedroom?

A hollow laugh rose and died in her throat as she preceded Diego into the house.

'Would you like something to drink?' He undid his tie and unbuttoned his jacket.

Cassandra continued towards the stairs. 'Play *pretend*?' She reached the elegantly curved balustrade and began ascending the stairs. 'In order to put a different context on the reason I'm here?'

'A man and a woman well-matched in bed?' Diego countered silkily, and she paused to turn and face him.

'It's just…sex.' And knew she lied.

Without a further word she moved towards the upper floor, aware of the sensual anticipation building with every step she took.

The warmth, the heat and the passion of his possession became a palpable entity, and she hated herself for wanting what he could gift her, for there was a part of her that wanted it to be real. The whole emotional package, not just physical sex.

Yet sex was all it could be. And she should be glad. To become emotionally involved with Diego would be akin to leaping from a plane without a parachute.

Death-defying, exhilarating…madness.

Cassandra made her way along the gallery to the

main bedroom, and once there she stepped out of her stiletto-heeled pumps, removed her jewellery, then reached for the zip fastener of her gown.

She was aware of Diego's presence in the room, and the fact he'd retrieved her overnight bag. Her fingers shook a little as she took it from him and retreated into the *en suite*.

Minutes later she removed her make-up, then she unpinned her hair and deliberately avoided checking her mirrored image.

Showtime.

Diego was reclining in bed, his upper body propped up on one elbow, looking, she perceived wryly, exactly what he was…one very sexy and dangerous man.

She was suddenly supremely conscious of the large T-shirt whose hemline fell to mid-thigh, her tumbled hair and freshly scrubbed face.

The antithesis of glamour. Alicia, or any one of the many women who had shared his bed, would have elected to wear something barely-there, probably transparent, in black or scarlet. Provocative, titillating, and guaranteed to raise a certain part of the male anatomy.

Except she wasn't here to provoke or titillate, and she slid beneath the covers, settled them in place, then turned her head to look at him.

He lifted a hand and trailed fingers across her cheek, then threaded his fingers through her hair.

He traced the delicate skin beneath her ear, then

circled the hollow at the base of her neck as he fastened his mouth over hers.

She told herself she was in control, that this was just physical pleasure without any emotional involvement.

Only to stifle a groan in despair as his hand slid down her body to rest on her thigh.

How could she succumb so easily? It galled her to think she'd been on tenterhooks all evening, waiting for this moment, *wanting* it.

His tongue tangled with hers in an erotic dance as she began to respond. Her T-shirt no longer provided a barrier, and she exulted in the glide of his hands as he moulded her body close to his.

Diego rolled onto his back, carrying her with him, and he eased her against the cradle of his thighs, then shaped her breasts, weighing them gently as he caressed the sensitive skin.

Their peaks hardened beneath his touch, and the breath hissed between her teeth as he rolled each nub between thumb and forefinger, creating a friction that sent sensation soaring through her body.

With care he eased her forward to savour each peak in turn, and she cried out as he took her to the edge between pleasure and pain.

His arousal was a potent force, and he settled her against its thickened length, creating a movement that had the breath hitching in her throat.

Cassandra felt as if she was on fire, caught up in the passion he was able to evoke, rendering everything to a primitive level as he positioned her to accept him in a long, slow slide that filled her to the hilt.

Then he began to move, gently at first, governing her body to create a timeless rhythm that started slow and increased in depth and pace until she became lost, totally. Unaware of the sounds she uttered as she became caught up in the eroticism of scaling the heights, only to be held at the edge…and caught as she fell.

CHAPTER FIVE

IT WAS early when Cassandra stirred into wakefulness, the dawn providing a dull light filtering
through the drapes, and she lay there quietly for a
while before slipping from the bed.

With slow, careful movements she collected her
bag and trod quietly from the room, choosing to
dress at the end of the hallway before descending
the stairs to the kitchen, where she spooned ground
coffee into the coffee maker, filled the carafe with
water, then switched it on.

When it filtered, she took down a mug and filled
it, added sugar, and carried it out onto the terrace.

A new day, she mused, noting the glistening dew.
The sun was just lifting above the horizon, lighten-
ing the sky to a pale azure, and there was the faint
chirping of birds in nearby trees.

It was peaceful at this hour of the morning.
Nothing much stirred. There wasn't so much as a
breeze, and no craft moved in the harbour.

'You're awake early,' Diego drawled from the
open doorway, and she turned to look at him.

He was something else. Tousled dark hair, hastily
donned jeans barely snapped, bare-chested, nothing
on his feet...gone was the sophisticated image, in-

stead there was something primitive about his stance.

'I didn't mean to disturb you.'

Diego effected a faint shrug. 'I woke as you left the room.'

The memory of what they'd shared through the night was hauntingly vivid, and she swallowed the faint lump that rose in her throat. 'I'd like to leave soon. I have a few things to do, and I need to spend time with my father.'

'I'll start breakfast.'

'No. Please don't on my account. I'll just finish my coffee, then I'll get my bag.'

Suiting words to action, she drained the mug, then she moved through the house to the front door, collected her bag, and turned to say goodbye.

He was close, and she was unprepared for the brief hard kiss he pressed against her mouth.

Cassandra wasn't capable of uttering a word as he opened the door, and she moved quickly down to her car, slipped in behind the wheel, fired the engine, then she eased the Porsche down the driveway.

There were the usual household chores, and she spent time checking her electronic mail before leaving to visit her father.

His increasing frailty concerned her, and she didn't stay long. He needed to rest, and she conferred with Cameron as to who would contact Alexander's cardiologist.

An early night was on the agenda, and she slept well, waking at the sound of the alarm to rise and face the day.

An early-morning meeting to review the week's agenda, assess supplies and prioritise work took place within minutes of her arrival, then she took position at her workspace and adjusted the binocular microscope to her satisfaction.

It was almost midday when her cellphone buzzed, signalling an incoming text message, and she retrieved it to smile with delight at the printed text. 'home, dinner when, news. Siobhan'

For those with minimum spare time and a tight schedule, text messaging provided easy communication. Brief, Cassandra grinned as she keyed in a response, but efficient.

Within minutes they'd organised a time and place to meet that evening.

Suddenly the day seemed brighter, and she found herself humming lightly beneath her breath as she adjusted a magnification instrument, then transferred to a correction loupe. Using a calliper, she focused on the intricate work in hand.

It was almost seven when Cassandra stepped into the trendy café. Superb food, excellent service, it was so popular bookings needed to be made in advance.

A waiter showed her to a table, and she ordered mineral water, then perused the menu while she waited for Siobhan to arrive.

She was able to tell the moment Siobhan entered the café. Almost in unison every male head turned towards the door, and everything seemed to stop for a few seconds.

Cassandra sank back in her chair and watched the effect, offering a quizzical smile as Siobhan extended an affectionate greeting.

'Cassy, sorry I'm late. Parking was a bitch.'

Very few people shortened her name, except Siobhan who used it as an endearment and fiercely corrected anyone who thought to follow her example.

The clothes, the long blonde flowing hair, exquisite but minimum make-up, the perfume. Genes, Siobhan blithely accorded, whenever anyone enviously queried how she managed to look the way she did. One of the top modelling agencies had snapped her up at fifteen, and she was treading the international catwalks in Rome, Milan and Paris two years later.

Yet for all the fame and fortune, none of it had gone to her head. On occasion she played the expected part, acquiring as she termed it, the *model* persona.

Together, they'd shared private schools and formed a friendship bond that was as true now as it had been then.

Siobhan barely had time to slip into a seat before a waiter appeared at her side, and she gave him her order.

'Mineral water. Still.'

The poor fellow was so enraptured he could hardly speak, and barely refrained from genuflecting before he began to retreat.

Cassandra bit back a smile as she sank back in her seat. 'How was Italy?'

'The catwalk, behind-the-scene diva contretemps, or the most divine piece of jewellery I acquired?'

'Jewellery,' she said promptly, and gave an appreciative murmur of approval as Siobhan indicated the diamond tennis bracelet at her wrist. Top-grade stones, bezel setting…exquisite. 'Beautiful. A gift?'

'From me to me.' Siobhan grinned. 'Otherwise known as retail therapy.'

Cassandra gave a delighted laugh. 'Moving on…tell me about the Italian count.'

'Sustenance first, Cassy, darling. I'm famished.'

It wasn't fair that Siobhan could eat a healthy serving of almost anything and still retain the fabulous svelte form required by the world's top designers to model their clothes.

Cassandra made a selection, while Siobhan did likewise, and another waiter appeared to take their order the instant Siobhan lowered the menu.

'Dining with you is an incredible experience,' Cassandra said with an impish grin. 'The waiters fall over themselves just for the pleasure of fulfilling your slightest whim.'

Siobhan's eyes twinkled with devilish humour. 'Helpful when things are hectic, and I have like—'

she gestured with her glass '—five minutes to take a food break.' Her cellphone rang, and she ignored it.

'Shouldn't you get that?'

'No.'

'O-K,' she drew out slowly. 'You're not taking phone calls in general, or not from one person in particular?'

'The latter.'

Their chicken Caesar salads arrived and were placed before them with a stylish flourish.

'Problems?' Cassandra ventured.

'Some,' Siobhan admitted, and sipped from her glass.

'The Italian count?'

'The Italian count's ex-wife.'

Oh, my. 'She doesn't want you to have him?'

'Got it in one.' Siobhan picked up her cutlery and speared a piece of chicken.

'You're not going to fill in the gaps?'

'She wants to retain her title by marriage.' Siobhan's eyes rolled. 'Lack of social face, and all that crap.'

'You don't care a fig about the title.' It was a statement, not a query.

'They share joint custody of their daughter. The ex is threatening to change the custody arrangements.'

'Can she do that?'

'By questioning my ability to provide reasonable

care and attention while the child is in the paternal home due to my occupation and lifestyle.'

'Ouch,' she managed in sympathy.

'Aside from that, Rome was wonderful. The fashion showing went well…out front,' she qualified. 'Out back one of the models threw a hissy fit, and was soothed down only seconds before she was due to hit the catwalk.' She leaned forward, and made an expressive gesture with her fork. 'Your turn.'

Where did she begin? Best not to even start, for how could she justify complex and very personal circumstances?

'The usual.' She effected a light shrug. 'Nothing much changes.'

'Word has it you and Diego del Santo are an item.'

Ah, the speed of the social grapevine! 'We were guests at a dinner party, and attended the same gallery exhibition.'

'Cassy, this is *me*, remember? Being fellow guests at the same event is something you've done for the past year. It's a step up to arrive and leave with him.'

'A step up, huh?'

'So,' Siobhan honed in with a quizzical smile. *'Tell.'*

'It seemed a good idea at the time,' she responded lightly. It was part truth, and the model's gaze narrowed.

'You're hooked.'

'Not in this lifetime.'

'Uh-huh.'

'You're wrong,' Cassandra denied. 'He's—'

'One hell of a man,' Siobhan finished, and her expressive features softened. 'Well, I'll be damned.'

A delighted laugh escaped her lips as she lifted her glass and touched its rim to the one Cassandra held. 'Good luck, Cassy, darling.'

Luck? All she wanted was for the next week to be over and done with!

They finished their meal and lingered over coffee, parting well after ten with the promise to catch up again soon.

Thursday morning Cassandra woke when the cat began to miaow in protest at not being fed, and she rolled over to check the time, saw the digital blinking, and muttered an unladylike oath. A power failure during the night had wiped out her alarm, and she scrambled for her wrist-watch to check the time…only to curse again and leap from the bed.

It didn't make a good start to the day.

Minutes later she heard the dull burr of the phone from the *en suite* and opted to let the machine pick up, rather than dash dripping wet from the shower.

Towelled dry, she quickly dressed, collected a cereal bar and a banana to eat as she drove to work, caught up her briefcase, and was almost to the door before she remembered to run the machine.

Cameron's recorded voice relayed he had tickets

to a gala film première that evening, and asked her to return his call.

She'd planned a quiet night at home, but her brother enjoyed the social scene and she rarely refused any of his invitations. Besides, an evening out would help her forget Diego for a few hours.

As if.

His image intruded into every waking thought, intensifying as each day went by. As to the nights…they were worse, much worse. He'd begun to invade her dreams, and she'd wake mid-sequence to discover the touch of his mouth, his hands, was only a figment of an over-active imagination.

She cursed beneath her breath as she waited for the lift to take her down to the basement car park. Whatever gave her the idea she could enter into Diego's conditional arrangement and escape emotionally unscathed?

Fighting peak-hour traffic merely added to her overall sense of disquiet, and it was mid-morning before she managed to return Cameron's call.

The workshop prided itself on producing quality work, and there was satisfaction in achieving an outstanding piece. Especially a commissioned item where the designer had worked with the client in the selection of gems and setting.

Software made it possible to assemble a digital diagram, enhance and produce an example of the finished piece.

There was real challenge in producing something

strikingly unusual, even unique, where price was no object. Occasionally frustration played a part when the client insisted on a design the jeweller knew wouldn't display the gems to their best advantage.

It was almost six when she let herself into the apartment, and she fed the cat, watered her plants, then showered and dressed for the evening ahead.

On a whim she selected an elegant black trouser suit, added a red pashmina, and slid her feet into stiletto-heeled sandals. Upswept hair, skilful use of make-up, and she was ready just as Cameron buzzed through his arrival on the intercom.

The venue was Fox Studios, the film's lead actors had jetted in from the States, and Australian actors of note would attend as guests of honour, Cameron informed as they approached the studios.

Together they made their way into the crowded foyer, where guests mingled as waiters offered champagne and orange juice.

The film was predicted to be a box-office success, with special effects advertised as surpassing anything previously seen on screen.

There was the usual marketing pizzazz, the buzz of conversation, and Cassandra recognised a few fellow guests as she stood sipping champagne.

'I imagine Diego will be here tonight.'

'Possibly,' she conceded with deliberate unconcern, aware that if he did attend it was unlikely to be alone.

'Does that bother you?'

'Why should it? He's a free agent.' The truth shouldn't hurt so much. 'I'm just a transitory issue he decided to amuse himself with.'

She didn't want to see him here…or anywhere else for that matter. It would merely accentuate the difference between their public lives and the diabolical arrangement Diego had made in forcing her to be part of a deal.

'He's just arrived,' Cameron indicated quietly.

'Really?' Pretending indifference was a practised art, and she did it well. She told herself she wouldn't indulge in an idle glance of the foyer's occupants, only to have her attention drawn as if by a powerful magnet to where Diego stood.

Attired in an immaculate evening suit, he looked every inch the powerful magnate. Blatant masculinity and elemental ruthlessness made for a dangerous combination in any arena.

Cassandra's gaze fused with his, and in that moment she was prepared to swear everything stood still.

Sensation swirled through her body, tuning it to a fine pitch as she fought to retain a measure of composure.

Almost as if he knew, he inclined his head in acknowledgement and proffered a faintly mocking smile before returning his attention to the man at his side.

It was then Cassandra saw Alicia move into his

circle, and she felt sickened by Alicia's effusive greeting.

With deliberate movements she positioned herself so Diego was no longer in her line of vision, and she initiated an animated conversation with Cameron about the merits of German and Italian motor engineering.

Cars numbered high on his list of personal obsessions, and he launched into a spiel of detailed data that went right over her head.

He was in his element, and she allowed her mind to drift as she tuned out his voice.

Diego didn't owe her any loyalty. If he'd issued her with an invitation to partner him here tonight, she would have refused. So why did she care?

Logic and rationale were fine, but they did nothing to ease the pain in the vicinity of her heart.

Are you crazy? she demanded silently. You don't even *like* him. Why let him get to you? Except it was too late…way too late. He was already there.

'…and given a choice, I'd opt for Ferrari,' Cameron concluded, only to quizzically ask, 'Have you heard a word I said?'

'It was an interesting comparison,' Cassandra inclined with a faint smile.

'Darling, don't kid yourself. You were miles away.' He paused for a few seconds, then said gently, 'Alicia isn't *with* him. She's just trying to make out she is.'

'I really don't care.'

'Yes, you do. And that worries me.'

'Don't,' she advised with soft vehemence. 'I went into this with my eyes open.'

'There's only the weekend, then it's over.'

Now, why did that send her into a state of mild despair?

It was a relief when the auditorium doors opened and the guests moved forward to await direction to their seats.

'Cassandra. Cameron.'

She'd have recognised that faintly accented drawl anywhere, and she summoned a polite smile as she turned towards the man who'd joined them.

'Diego,' she acknowledged, and watched as he shifted his gaze to Cameron.

'If I had known you were attending I could have arranged a seating reallocation.'

'I was gifted the tickets last night,' Cameron relayed with regret.

'Pity.'

Alicia appeared at Diego's side, and curved her arm sinuously through his own. 'Diego, we're waiting for you.' She made a pretence of summoning charm. 'Cassandra, Cameron. I'm sure you'll excuse us?'

Diego deliberately released her arm from his, and Cassandra wondered if she was the only one who caught the dangerous glitter in Alicia's eyes.

To compound the situation, Diego ushered Cassandra and Cameron ahead, and Cassandra felt

Alicia's directed venom like hot knives piercing her back.

'That was interesting,' Cameron accorded quietly as they slid into their seats. 'Alicia is a first-class bitch.'

'They deserve each other,' Cassandra declared with dulcet cynicism, and incurred a musing glance.

'Darling, Diego is light-years ahead of her.'

'Is that meant as a compliment or a condemnation?'

Cameron laughed out loud. 'I'll opt for the former. I'm sure you prefer the latter.'

Wasn't that the truth!

The film proved to be a riveting example of superb technical expertise with hand-to-the-throat suspense that had the audience gasping in their seats.

Eventually the credits rolled, the lights came on, and guests began vacating the theatre.

Cassandra sent up a silent prayer she'd manage to escape without encountering Diego. Except the deity wasn't listening, and the nerves inside her stomach accelerated as he drew level with them in the foyer.

His gaze locked with hers, and she could read nothing from his expression. 'We're going on for coffee, if you'd care to join us.'

Are you kidding? You expect me to sit opposite you, calmly sipping a latte, while Alicia plays the vamp?

'Thank you, no,' she got in quickly before

Cameron had a chance to accept. 'I have an early start in the morning.' She didn't, but he wasn't to know that, and she offered a sweet smile as he inclined his head.

'I'll be in touch.'

Alicia's mouth tightened, and Cassandra glimpsed something vicious in those ice-blue eyes for a timeless second, then it was gone.

Cassandra wasn't conscious of holding her breath until Diego moved ahead of them, then she released it slowly, conscious of Cameron's soft exclamation as she did so.

'Watch your back with that one, darling,' he cautioned. 'Alicia has it in for you.'

She met her brother's wry look with equanimity. 'Tell me something I don't know.'

They reached the exit and began walking towards where Cameron had parked the car. 'If she discovers Diego is sleeping with you...' He left the sentence unfinished.

'I can look after myself.'

He caught hold of her hand and squeezed it in silent reassurance. 'Just take care, OK?'

CHAPTER SIX

'CASSANDRA, phone.'

Diego, it had to be.

Cassandra took the call, and tried to control the way her pulse leapt at the sound of his voice.

'We're taking the mid-morning flight. I'll collect you at nine tomorrow.'

'I can meet you at the airport.' That way her car would be there when they returned.

'Nine, Cassandra,' he reiterated in a quiet drawl that brooked little argument, then he cut the connection.

He was insufferable, she fumed as she returned to her workspace.

The resentment didn't diminish much as day became night, and she rose early, packed, put out sufficient dry food and water for the cat, then a few minutes before nine she took the lift down to Reception.

The Gold Coast appeared at its sparkling best. Clear azure sky, late-spring warm temperatures, and sunshine.

Diego picked up a hire car and within half an hour they reached the luxurious Palazzo Versace hotel complex.

It was more than a year since Cassandra had last visited the Coast, and she adored the holiday atmosphere, the canal estates, the trendy sidewalk café's and casual lifestyle.

The hotel offered six-star accommodation, plus privately owned condominiums and several penthouse apartments.

Why should she be surprised to discover Diego owned a penthouse here? Or that he'd elected to take the extra total designer furnishing package including bed coverings and cushions, towels, china, glassware and cutlery?

The total look, she mused in admiration. Striking, expensive, and incredibly luxurious.

There was a million-dollar view from the floor-to-ceiling glass walls, and she took a deep breath of fresh sea air as Diego slid open an external glass door.

Delightful. But let's not forget the reason he's brought you here, an imp taunted silently.

Bedroom duties. The thought should have filled her with antipathy, but instead there was a sense of anticipation at a raw primitive level to experience again the magical, mesmeric excitement he was able to evoke.

Was it so wrong to want his touch, his possession without any emotional involvement other than the pleasure of the moment?

Don't kid yourself, she chided inwardly. Like it

or not, you're involved right up to your slender neck!

After this weekend her life would return to normal...*whatever* normal meant. Work, she mused as Diego took their overnight bags through to the bedroom. The usual social activities...which would never be quite the same again as she encountered Diego partnering Alicia, or any one of several other women all too willing to share his evening. Dammit, his *bed*.

How would she cope, imagining that muscular male body engaged in the exchange of sexual body fluids? The entanglement of limbs, the erotic pleasure of his mouth savouring warm feminine skin as he sought each sensual hollow, every intimate crevice?

It would be killing, she admitted silently. Perhaps she could retreat into living the life of a social recluse, and simply bury herself in work.

Except that would be accepting defeat, and she refused to contemplate a slide into negativity.

For now, there was the day, and she intended to make the most of it. With or without him. The night he would claim as his, but meantime...

Cassandra heard him re-enter the spacious lounge, and she lifted a hand and gestured to the view out over the Broadwater. 'It's beautiful here.'

Diego moved to stand behind her, and she was supremely conscious of him. Her skin tingled in reaction to his body warmth, and the temptation to lean back against him was almost irresistible.

'Do you spend much time here?' It seemed almost a sacrilege to leave the apartment empty for long periods of time.

'The occasional weekend,' he drawled.

But not often, she concluded, and wondered if and when he took a break to enjoy the fruits of his success. He possessed other homes, in other countries...perhaps he chose somewhere more exotic where he could relax and unwind.

'Lunch,' Diego indicated. 'We can eat in the restaurant here, cross the road to the Sheraton Hotel, or explore nearby Tedder Avenue.'

She turned towards him and saw he'd exchanged tailored trousers for shorts, and joggers replaced hand-tooled leather shoes.

'You're allowing me to choose?'

'Don't be facetious,' he chided gently.

'Tedder Avenue,' Cassandra said without hesitation. 'We can walk there.' Half a kilometre was no distance at all.

One eyebrow rose in quizzical humour. 'You want exercise, I can think of something more athletic.'

'Ah, but my sexual duties don't begin until dark...remember?'

He pressed an idle finger to the lower curve of her lip. 'A sassy mouth could get you into trouble.'

'In that case, I'll freshen up and we can leave.'

His husky laugh curled around her nerve-ends, pulled a little, then she stepped around him and walked through to the master bedroom.

She took a few minutes to change into tailored shorts and blouse, then she snagged a cap, her shoulder bag, and re-entered the lounge.

'Let's hit the road.'

It was a pleasant walk, the warmth of the sun tempered by a light breeze, and they settled on one of several pavement cafés, ordered, then ate with evident enjoyment.

They were almost ready to leave when Diego's cellphone buzzed, and she looked askance when he merely checked the screen and didn't pick up.

'It'll go to message-bank.'

'Perhaps you should take that,' Cassandra said when it buzzed again a few minutes later.

Diego merely shrugged and ignored a further insistent summons.

Within a few minutes Cassandra's cellphone buzzed from inside her bag, and she retrieved it, saw the unfamiliar number displayed, then engaged the call.

'You're with Diego.' The feminine voice was tight with anger. 'Aren't you?'

Oh, lord. 'Alicia?'

'He's taken you to the Coast for the weekend, hasn't he?'

'What makes you think that?'

'Fundamental mathematics.'

'No chance you might be wrong?'

'Darling, I've already checked. Diego picked you up from your apartment this morning.'

Counting to ten wouldn't do it. Hell, even *twenty* wouldn't come close. 'You have a problem,' Cassandra managed evenly.

'*You* in Diego's life is the problem.'

'I suggest you discuss it with him.'

'Oh, I intend to.'

She cut the connection and met Diego's steady gaze with equanimity. 'You owe Alicia an explanation.'

'No,' he said quietly. 'I don't.'

'She seems to think you do.'

The waitress presented the bill, which he paid, adding a tip, then when she left he sank back in his chair and subjected Cassandra to an unwavering appraisal.

'Whatever Alicia and I shared ended several months ago.'

She raised an eyebrow and offered him a cynical smile. 'Yet you continue to date her?'

'We have mutual friends, we receive the same invitations.' He lifted his shoulders in a negligible shrug. 'Alicia likes to give the impression we retain a friendship.'

She couldn't help herself. 'Something she manages to do very well.'

Diego's eyes hardened. 'That bothers you?'

'Why should it?'

Did she think he was oblivious to the way her pulse quickened whenever he moved close? Or feel the thud of her heart? The soft warmth colouring her skin, or the way her eyes went dark an instant before his mouth found hers?

'It's over, and Alicia needs to move on.'

A chill slithered down her spine. As she would have to move on come Monday? What was she *thinking*, for heaven's sake? She couldn't wait for the weekend to be over so she could get on with her life.

A life in which Diego didn't figure at all.

Now, why did that thought leave her feeling strangely bereft?

'Let's walk along the beach,' Cassandra suggested as they stood to their feet. She had the sudden need to feel the golden sand beneath her feet, the sun on her skin, and the peace and tranquillity offered by a lazy outgoing tide.

The ocean lay a block distant, and within minutes she slid off her sandals and padded down to the damp, packed sand at the water's edge.

They wandered in companionable silence, admiring the long, gentle curve stretching down towards Kirra. Tall, high-rise apartment buildings in varying height and colour dotted the foreshore, and there was a fine haze permeating the air.

Children played in the shallows while parents stood guard, and in the distance seagulls hovered, seemingly weightless, before drifting slowly down onto the sand to dig their beaks in in search of a tasty morsel.

It was a peaceful scene which changed and grew more crowded as they neared Surfer's Paradise.

'Feel like exploring the shops?' Diego ventured, and Cassandra inclined her head.

'Brave of you. That's tantamount to giving a woman *carte blanche*.'

'Perhaps I feel in an indulgent mood.'

'Who would refuse?' she queried lightly, and changed direction, pausing as they reached the board-walk to brush sand from her feet before slipping on her sandals.

It became a delightful afternoon as they strolled along an avenue housing several designer boutiques before venturing down another where Cassandra paused to examine some fun T-shirts.

She selected one and took it to the salesgirl, whereupon Diego extracted his wallet and passed over a bill.

'No.' Cassandra waved his hand aside, and shot him an angry glance as he insisted, to the amusement of the salesgirl, who doubtless thought Cassandra a graceless fool. 'Thank you, but no,' she reiterated firmly as she forcibly placed her own bill into the salesgirl's hand.

She was the first woman who'd knocked back his offer to pay, and her fierce independence amused him. There had been a time when he'd had to watch every cent and look to handouts for clothing and food. Nor was he particularly proud he'd resorted to sleight-of-hand on occasion. Very few knew he now donated large sums of money each year to shelters for the homeless, and funded activity centres for underprivileged children.

'Let's take a break and linger over a latte,' Diego suggested as they emerged from the shop.

'Can't hack the pace, huh?' Cassandra teased as she tucked her fingers through the plastic carry-bag containing her purchase.

There wasn't an ounce of spare flesh on that powerful body, and she wondered what he did to keep fit.

A gym? Perhaps a personal trainer?

They took a cab back to the Palazzo as dusk began to fall, and on entering the penthouse Cassandra headed for the bedroom, where she gathered up a change of clothes and made for the *en suite*.

There was a necessity to shampoo the salt-mist from her hair, and she combined it with a leisurely shower, then she emerged from the glass stall, grabbed a bath-towel and she had just secured it sarong-style when Diego walked naked into the *en suite*.

Oh, my, was all that came immediately to mind. Superb musculature, olive skin, a light smattering of dark, curly hair on his chest. Broad shoulders, a tapered waist, slim hips…

She forced her appraisal to halt there, unable to

let it travel lower for fear of how it would affect her composure.

It was difficult to meet his gaze, and she didn't even try. Instead she moved past him and entered the bedroom, sure of his faint husky chuckle as she closed the door behind her.

There was a certain degree of satisfaction in witnessing her discomfort. In truth, it delighted him to know she wasn't entirely comfortable with him, and there was pleasure in the knowledge her experience with men was limited.

His body reacted at the thought of the night ahead. Her scent, the taste of her skin…*por Dios,* how it felt to be inside her.

He hadn't felt quite this sense of anticipation for a woman since his early teens when raging hormones made little distinction between one girl or another.

Now there was desire and passion for one woman, only one. Cassandra.

If he had his way, he'd towel himself dry, go into the bedroom and initiate a night-long seduction she'd never forget.

Soon, he promised himself as he turned the water dial from hot to cold. But first, they'd dine at the restaurant downstairs overlooking the pool. Fine wine, good food.

Cassandra put the finishing touches to her make-up, then she caught up an evening purse and preceded Diego from the apartment.

The classic black gown with its lace overlay was suitable for any occasion. The very reason she'd packed it, together with black stiletto-heeled pumps. A long black lace scarf wound loosely at her neck was a stunning complement, and she wore minimum jewellery, diamond ear-studs and a diamond tennis bracelet.

With her hair twisted into an elegant knot atop her head, she looked the cool, confident young woman. Who was to know inside she was a mass of nerves?

Act, a tiny voice prompted. You can do it, you're good at it. Practised social graces. Taught in the very best of private schools.

The restaurant was well-patronised, and the *maître d'* presided with friendly formality as he saw them seated.

Wine? One glass, which she sipped throughout the meal, and, although they conversed, she had little recollection of the discussion.

For there was only the man, and the sexual aura he projected. It was a powerful aphrodisiac…primitive, *lethal*.

She had only to look at his hands to recall the magic they created as they stroked her skin. And his mouth…the passion it evoked in her was to die for, almost literally.

For she did die a little with each orgasm as he led her towards a tumultuous climax and joined her at the peak, held her there, before toppling them both in glorious free-fall.

The mere thought sent the blood racing through her veins, the quickened thud of her heartbeat audible to her ears as she waited for the moment Diego would settle the bill.

How long had the meal lasted? Two hours, three? She had little recollection of the passage of time.

The apartment was dark when they returned, and Cassandra crossed to the wall of glass to admire the night-scape.

The water resembled a dark mass, dappled by threads of reflected light. Bright neon flashed on buildings across the Broadwater, and there were distant stars dotting an indigo sky.

She sensed rather than heard Diego stand behind her, and she made no protest as he cupped each shoulder and drew her back against him.

His lips caressed the delicate hollows at the edge of her neck, and sensation curled deep within, radiating in a sweet, heated circle through her body until she felt achingly alive.

Diego slid a hand down to grasp hers, and he led her down to the bedroom. He dimmed the lights down low, then slowly removed each article of her clothing until she stood naked before him. With care he lifted both hands to her hair and slowly removed the pins, so its length cascaded down onto her shoulders.

He traced a pattern over her breasts, then drew a

line down to her belly before seeking the moist heart of her.

'You're wearing too many clothes,' she managed shakily, and watched as he divested each one of them.

Then he lowered his head and kissed her, arousing such passion she soon lost a sense of time or place as she became lost in the man, a wanton willing to gift and take sensual pleasure until there could be only one end.

It was then Diego pulled her down onto the bed and ravished her with such exquisite slowness she cried out in demand he assuage the ache deep within.

Afterwards they slept, to wake at dawn to indulge in the slow, sweet loving of two people in perfect sexual accord.

It was an idyllic place, Cassandra bestowed wistfully as they sat eating breakfast out by the pool, and wondered how it would feel to fall asleep in Diego's arms every night, knowing he was *there*. To gift him pleasure, as he pleasured her.

Whoa…wait a minute here. So the sex is great. Hell, let's go with fantastic. But it stops with to-night.

Early tomorrow morning they'd take the dawn flight back to Sydney and go their separate ways.

She should be happy it was nearly over. Instead she felt incredibly bereft.

Given the option of how to spend the day,

Cassandra chose the theme park. Lots of people, plenty of entertainment, and it meant she didn't have much opportunity to dwell on the coming night.

Tigers, baby cubs, the Imax theatre were only a few of the features available, and the hours slipped by with gratifying ease.

'Want to dine out, or order in?' Diego queried as they returned to the penthouse.

'Order in.' It would be nice to sit out on the balcony beneath dimmed lighting, sip chilled wine, and sample food while taking in the night scene out over the marina, where large cruisers lay at berth and people wandered along the adjacent board-walk.

He moved to where she stood and trailed light fingers down her cheek. 'Simple pleasures, hmm?'

Sensation began to unfurl deep inside, increasing her pulse-beat. It was crazy. Think with your head, she bade silently. If you go with what your heart dictates, you'll be in big trouble. Somehow she had the feeling it was way too late for rationale.

'I'll go freshen up.' If she didn't move away from him, she'd be lost.

A refreshing shower did much to restore a sense of normalcy, and she donned jeans and a cotton-knit top, tied her hair back, then added a touch of lip-gloss.

Diego was standing in the lounge talking on his cellphone, and he concluded the call as she entered the room.

'Check the menu while I shower and change.'

Seafood, Cassandra decided as she viewed the selection offered, and chose prawn risotto with bruschetta. Diego, when he re-emerged in black jeans and polo shirt, endorsed her suggestion and added lobster tail and salad.

Diego opened a bottle of chilled sauvignon blanc while they waited for the food to be delivered, and they moved out on the balcony as the night sky began to deepen.

Lights became visible in a number of luxury cabin cruisers berthed close by, and Cassandra stilled, mesmerised, as Diego leant out a hand and freed the ribbon from her hair.

'All day I've resisted the temptation.' He threaded his fingers through its length so it curved down over her shoulders.

The breeze stirred the fine strands, tumbling them into a state of disarray. A warm smile curved his mouth as he leaned in close and took possession of her mouth in an exploratory open-mouthed kiss that teased and tantalised as he evoked her response.

He tasted of cool wine, and she placed a steadying hand to his shoulders and leaned in for a few brief moments until the electronic peal of the doorbell broke them apart.

Diego collected the restaurant food while Cassandra set the small balcony table with fine china and cutlery, and they shared a leisurely meal, offering each other forked morsels of food to sample in a gourmet feast.

The moon shone brightly, and there were myriad tiny stars sprinkling the night sky. Magical, she accorded silently.

They lingered over the wine, and when a fresh breeze started up they carried everything indoors, dealt with the few dishes, dispensed the food containers, and contemplated coffee.

It wasn't late, yet all it took was the drift of his fingers tracing the line of her slender neck, the touch of his lips at her temple, and she became lost.

With one fluid movement he swept her into his arms and carried her down to the bedroom, where dispensing with her clothes, his, became almost an art form.

She wanted to savour every moment, each kiss, the touch of his hands, his mouth, and exult in his possession. To gift him pleasure and hear the breath hiss between his teeth, his husky groan as she drove him to the end of his endurance.

When he reached it, she drew him in, the long, deep thrust plunging to the hilt, and he felt her warm, slick heat, revelled in the way she enclosed him, urging a hard, driving rhythm that scaled the heights with a shattering climax that left them both exhausted.

Afterwards they slept for a few hours, and Cassandra stirred as he carried her into the *en suite* and stepped into the spa-bath.

Dreamlike, she allowed his ministrations, and stood like an obedient child as he blotted the moisture from her body before tending to his own, then he took her back to bed to savour her body in a long, sweet loving that almost made her weep.

All too soon it was time to shower and dress, pack, drink strong black coffee, then drive down to Coolangatta Airport. Check-in time was disgustingly early, the flight south smooth and uneventful.

It was just after eight when they disembarked at Sydney Airport, and it took scant minutes to traverse the concourse to ground level.

'I'll take a cab,' Cassandra indicated as they emerged from the terminal.

Diego shot her a dark look that spoke volumes. 'Don't be ridiculous.'

'I need to get to work.'

One eyebrow slanted. 'So I'll drop you there.'

'It's out of your way.'

'What's that got to do with anything?'

She heaved an eloquent sigh. 'Diego—'

'Cool it, Cassandra. You're coming with me.'

Like a marionette when the puppeteer pulls the string? She opened her mouth to protest, only to close it again as the Aston Martin swept into the parking bay with an attendant at the wheel.

She remained silent during the drive into the city, and she had her seat belt undone with her hand on the door-clasp when he eased the car to a halt adjacent to the jewellery workshop.

'Thank you for a pleasant weekend.' The words sounded incredibly inadequate as she slid from the passenger seat. 'If you pop the trunk I'll collect my bag, then you won't need to get out of the car.'

Except her words fell on deaf ears as he emerged from behind the wheel, collected her bag and handed it to her.

Then he lowered his head and took possession of her mouth in a brief, hard kiss that left her gasping for breath. Then he released her and slid into the car as she walked away without so much as a backward glance.

Could anyone see her heart was breaking? Somehow she doubted it as she got on with the day. She checked with Sylvie, Alexander's nurse, and arranged to share dinner that evening with her father.

At four Cameron rang, jubilant with the news Diego had released the balance of funds.

Mission accomplished, she perceived grimly as she took a cab to her apartment, changed and freshened up, then she drove to Alexander's home.

He looked incredibly frail, and she felt her spirits plummet at the knowledge he'd deteriorated in the short time since she'd seen him last.

His appetite seemed to have vanished, and she coaxed him to eat, amusing him with anecdotes that brought forth a smile.

Cassandra stayed a while, sitting with him until Sylvie declared it was time for him to retire. Then she kissed his cheek and held him close for a few long minutes before taking her leave.

Meeting Diego's demands had been worth it.

Alexander remained ignorant of Cameron's business inadequacies, together with details surrounding his private life.

What about *you*? a tiny voice demanded a few hours later as she tossed and turned in her bed in search of sleep.

CHAPTER SEVEN

THURSDAY morning Cassandra woke with an uneasy feeling in the pit of her stomach. A premonition of some kind?

She slid out of bed, fed the cat, made a cup of tea and checked her emails, then she showered, dressed, and left for work.

There was nothing to indicate the day would be different from any other. Traffic was at its peak-hour worst, and an isolated road-rage incident, while momentarily disconcerting, didn't rattle her nerves overmuch.

Work progression proved normal, with nothing untoward occurring. Cameron rang, jubilant the Preston-Villers deal with Diego was a *fait accompli*, suggesting she join him for a celebration dinner.

So why couldn't she shake this sense of foreboding that hung around like a grey cloud?

It was almost six when she entered the apartment, and she greeted the cat, fed her, and was about to fix something to eat for herself when her cellphone buzzed.

'Cassandra.' Sylvie's voice sounded calm and unhurried. 'Alexander is being transported to hospital by ambulance. I'm about to follow. I've spoken to

119

Cameron, and he's already on his way.' She named the city's main cardiac unit. 'I'll see you there.'

Cassandra's stomach plummeted as she caught up her bag, her keys, and raced from the apartment. The cardiologist's warning returned to haunt her as she took the lift down to basement level, slid into her car to drive as quickly as traffic and the speed limit would allow.

Hospital parking was at a premium, and she brought her car to a screeching halt in a reserved space, hastily scrawled *emergency* onto a scrap of paper and slid it beneath the windscreen wiper, then she ran into the building.

What followed numbered among the worst hours of her life. Sylvie was there, waiting, and Cameron. The cardiac team were working to stabilise Alexander, but the prognosis wasn't good.

At midnight they sent Sylvie home, and Cassandra and Cameron kept vigil as the long night crept slowly towards dawn.

'Go home, get some sleep,' Cameron bade gently, and she shook her head.

At nine they each made calls, detailing the reason neither would be reporting for work, and took alternate one-hour shifts at Alexander's bedside.

It was there Diego found her, looking pale, wan and so utterly saddened it was all he could do not to sweep her into his arms and hold her close.

Not that she'd thank him for it, he perceived, aware he had no place here. Strict *family only* regulations applied, but he'd managed to circumvent them in order to gain a few minutes to express regret and ask if there was anything he could do.

'No,' Cassandra said quietly. 'Thank you.'

Diego cupped her shoulder, allowed his hand to linger there before letting it fall to his side.

A hovering nurse cast him a telling look, indicated the time, and he inclined his head in silent acquiescence.

'I'll keep in touch.'

'How did he get in here?' Cassandra asked quietly minutes later, and Cameron responded wearily,

'By sheer strength of will, I imagine. It happens to be one of his characteristics, or hadn't you noticed?'

In spades, she acknowledged, then jerked to startled attention as the machines monitoring her father's vital signs began an insistent beeping.

From then on it was all downhill, and Alexander slipped away from them late that evening.

Cassandra lapsed into a numbed state, and both she and Cameron shared a few silent tears in mutual consolation.

'Maybe you should spend the night at my place.'

She pulled away from him and searched for a handkerchief. 'I'll be fine. I just want to have a shower and fall into bed.'

'That goes for me, too.'

They walked down the corridor to the lift and took it down to ground level, then emerged into the late-night air. Cameron saw her to the car, waited until she was seated, then leaned in. 'I'll follow and make sure you get home OK.'

At this hour the streets carried minimal traffic, and as she reached Double Bay a light shower of rain began to fall. She saw the headlights of Cameron's car at her rear, and as she turned in to her apartment building he sounded his horn, then executed a semicircle and disappeared from sight.

Weariness hit her as she stepped out of the lift, and she was so caught up in reflected thought she didn't see the tall male figure leaning against the wall beside her apartment door.

'Diego? What—?'

He reached out and extricated the keys from her fingers, unlocked the door and gently pushed her inside.

'—are you doing?' she finished tiredly. 'You shouldn't be here.'

'No?' He removed her shoulder bag, put it down on the side-table, then led her towards the kitchen. He made tea, invaded her fridge and put a sandwich together.

'Eat.'

Food? 'I don't feel like anything.'

'A few mouthfuls will do.'

It was easier to capitulate than argue, and she obediently took a bite, sipped the tea, then she pushed the plate away. Any more and she'd be physically ill.

'Shower and bed,' Cassandra relayed wearily as she stood to her feet. 'You can let yourself out.' She didn't bother to wait for him to answer. Didn't care to see if he stayed. It was all too much, and more than anything she needed to sleep.

Diego fed the cat, washed the few dishes, checked his cellphone, made one call, then he doused the lights and entered her bedroom.

She was already asleep, and he undressed, then carefully slid beneath the covers. The thought she might wake and weep with grief alone was a haunting possibility he refused to condone.

Cassandra was dreaming. Strong arms held her close, and she felt a hand smoothing her hair. Lips brushed her temple, and she sank deeper into the dreamlike embrace, savouring the warmth of muscle and sinew beneath her cheek, the steady beat of a human heart.

It was comforting, reassuring, and she was content to remain there, cushioned in security, and loath to emerge and face the day's reality.

Except dreams didn't last, and she surfaced slowly through the veils of sleep to discover it was no dream.

'Diego?'

'I hope to hell you didn't think it could be anyone else,' he growled huskily, and met her startled gaze.

'I didn't want you to be alone.'

She tried to digest the implication, and found it too hard at this hour of the morning.

He watched as comprehension dawned on her pale features, saw the pain and glimpsed her attempt to deal with it.

'Want to talk?'

Cassandra shook her head, and held back the tears, hating the thought of breaking down in front of him.

'I'll go make coffee.' It would give him something to do with his hands, otherwise he would use them to haul her close, and while his libido was high, he was determined the next time they made love it would be without redress.

He slid from the bed, pulled on trousers and a shirt, then he entered the *en suite*, only to re-emerge minutes later, wryly aware a woman's razor was no substitute for a man's electric shaver.

In the kitchen he ground fresh coffee beans, replaced a filter, and switched on the coffee maker.

It was after eight, and breakfast was a viable option. Eggs, ham, cheese...ingredients he used to make two fluffy omelettes, then he slid bread into the toaster.

Cassandra dressed in jeans, added a blouse, then tended to her hair. She felt better after cleansing her face, and following her usual morning routine.

Not great, she assured her mirrored image, but OK. Sufficient to face the day and all it would involve.

The smell of fresh coffee, toast and something cooking teased her nostrils, and she entered the kitchen to find Diego dishing food onto two plates.

Her appetite didn't amount to much, but she ate half the omelette, some toast, and sipped her way through two cups of coffee.

'Shouldn't you be wherever it is you need to be at this hour of the morning?'

'Later,' Diego drawled, leaning back in his chair, satisfied she looked less fragile. 'When Cameron arrives, I'll leave.'

Her eyes clouded a little. 'I'm OK.'

One eyebrow slanted. 'I wasn't aware I implied you weren't.'

The cat hopped up onto her lap, padded a little, then settled.

She owed him thanks. 'It was thoughtful of you to stay.'

'I had Cameron's word he'd contact me if you insisted on returning home.'

Diego had done that out of concern? For her?

At that moment the phone rang, and she answered it. Cameron was on his way over.

Cassandra began clearing the table, and they dealt with the dishes together. There was an exigent awareness she was loath to explore, and she concentrated on the job in hand.

When it was done, she used the pretext of tidying the bedroom to escape, and the intercom buzzed as she finished up.

Cameron didn't look as if he'd slept well, and she made fresh coffee, served it, and was unsure whether to be relieved or regretful when Diego indicated he would leave.

The days leading up to Alexander's funeral were almost as bleak as the funeral itself, and Cassandra took an extra day before returning to the jewellery workshop.

Sylvie stayed on at Alexander's home, Cameron flew to Melbourne on business, and Cassandra directed all her energy into work.

Diego rang, but she kept the conversations short for one reason or another and declined any invitation he chose to extend.

A pendant commissioned by Alicia would normally have had all the fine hairs on Cassandra's nape standing on end. As it was, she took extra care with the design, ensuring its perfection.

The ensuing days ran into a week, and Cameron returned to Sydney briefly before taking a flight interstate within days.

'Cassandra, you're wanted at the shop.'

She disengaged from the binocular microscope, ran a hand over the knot atop her head, then made her way towards the retail shop.

A client wanting advice on a design? Soliciting suggestions for a particular gem? Or someone who had admired one of her personal designs and wanted something similar?

Security was tight, and she went through the entry procedure, passed through the ante-room and entered the shop, where gems sparkled against dark velvet in various glass cabinets.

Two perfectly groomed assistants stood positioned behind glass counters, their facial expressions a polite mask as they regarded a tall young woman whose back and stance seemed vaguely familiar.

Then the woman swung round, and Cassandra saw why.

Alicia. Beautifully dressed, exquisitely made-up, and looking very much the international model.

Trouble was the word that immediately came to mind.

'Miss Vandernoot would like to discuss the pendant she commissioned.'

'Yes, of course,' Cassandra said politely and crossed to where Alicia stood. 'Perhaps you'd care to show it to me.' She reached for a length of jeweller's velvet and laid it on the glass counter top.

'This,' Alicia hissed as she all but tossed the pendant down.

It was a beautiful piece, rectangular in shape with five graduated diamonds set in gold. The attached chain, exquisite.

'There are scratches. And the diamonds are not the size and quality I originally settled on.'

It was exactly as Alicia had commissioned. The diamonds perfectly cut and set.

Cassandra extracted her loupe, and saw the

scratches at once. Several. None of which were there when Alicia inspected and took delivery of the pendant. Inflicted in a deliberate attempt to denigrate her expertise?

'My notes are on file,' she began politely, and she turned towards the senior assistant. 'Beverly, would you mind retrieving them? I need to check the original details with Miss Vandernoot.'

It took a while. Cassandra went through the design notations and instructions with painstaking thoroughness, taking time to clarify each point in turn, witnessed and checked with Beverly. By the time she finished, Alicia had nowhere to go.

'There's still the matter of the scratching.'

Cassandra could have wept at the desecration to what had been perfection. 'They can be removed,' she advised quietly.

Alicia drew herself up to her full height, which, aided by five-inch stiletto-heeled sandals, was more than impressive.

'I refuse to accept substandard workmanship.' She swept Cassandra's slender frame with a scathing look.

'If you care to leave the item, we'll assess the damage and repair it at no cost to you.'

'Restitution is the only acceptable solution,' Alicia demanded with haughty insolence. 'I want a full credit, and I get to keep the item.'

Cassandra had had enough. This wasn't about

jewellery. 'That's outrageous and against company policy,' she said quietly.

'If you don't comply, I'll report this to the jewellers' association and ensure it receives media attention.'

'Do that. Meanwhile we'll arrange an expert evaluation of the scratches by an independent jeweller, and his report will be run concurrently.'

She'd called Alicia's bluff, and left the model with no recourse whatsoever. Alicia knew it, and her expression wasn't pretty as she scooped up the pendant and chain and flung both into her bag.

With deceptive calm Cassandra turned towards Beverly. 'I'll see Miss Vandernoot out, shall I?'

It was a minor victory, but one that lasted only until they reached the street.

'Don't think you've won,' Alicia vented viciously. 'I want Diego, and I mean to have him.'

'Really?' Cassandra watched as the model's gaze narrowed measurably. 'Good luck.'

'Keep your hands off him. I've spent a lot of time and energy cultivating the relationship.'

For one wild moment, Cassandra thought Alicia was going to hit her, and she braced herself to deal with it, only to hear the model utter a few vehement oaths and walk away.

Settling back to work took effort, and she was glad when the day ended and she could go home.

Grief sat uneasily on her shoulders, and Alicia's hissy fit only served to exacerbate her emotions. It would be all too easy to rage against fate or sink into a well of tears.

What a choice, she decided as she let herself into her apartment. The cat ran up to her, and she crouched down to caress the velvet ears. A feline head butted her hand, then smooched appealingly before curling over onto its back in silent invitation for a tummy rub.

'Unconditional devotion,' she murmured as she obligingly rubbed the cat's fur, and heard the appreciative purr in response.

She was all alone with no one close to call.

Cameron was in Melbourne, Siobhan had returned to Italy, and she couldn't, *wouldn't* ring Diego.

OK, so she'd feed the cat, fix herself something to eat, then she'd clean the apartment. An activity that would take a few hours, after which she'd shower and fall into bed.

CHAPTER EIGHT

WORK provided a welcome panacea, and Cassandra applied herself diligently the following morning as she adjusted the binocular microscope and focused on the delicate setting. Its intricate design provided a challenge, professionally and personally.

She wanted the best, insisted on it, aware such attention to minuscule detail brought the desired result...perfection.

If achieving it meant working through a lunch-hour, or staying late at the workshop, nothing mattered except the quality of the work.

Yet there were safety precautions in place. Loose stones were easy to fence, and therefore provided a target for robbery. Priceless gems, expensive equipment. Security was tight, the vault one of the finest. Bulletproof glass shielded those who worked inside, and a high-priced security system took care of the rest.

It all added up to a heightened sense of caution. Something she had become accustomed to over the years, and one she never took for granted.

The cast-in-stone rule ensured two people, never one alone, occupied the workshop on the premise that if by chance something untoward happened to one, the other was able to raise the alarm.

In the three years she'd worked for this firm, no one had attempted to breach the security system in daylight.

Oh, for heaven's sake! Why were such thoughts chasing through her mind? Instinct, premonition? Or was it due to an acute vulnerability?

No matter how hard she tried, she was unable to dismiss Diego from her mind. He was an intrusive force, every waking minute of each day.

She could sense his touch without any trouble at all. *Feel* the way his mouth moved on her own. As to the rest of it…

Don't go there. The memories were too vivid, too intoxicating.

Great while it lasted, she admitted. A fleeting, transitory fling orchestrated for all the wrong reasons. Manipulation at its worst.

So why was she aching for him?

The deal was done. Preston-Villers would flourish beneath Diego's management. Cameron retained anonymity in his private life. As to her? She'd fulfilled all obligations and was off the hook.

A hollow laugh sounded low in her throat. Sure she was! She'd never been so tied up in her life!

She barely ate, she rarely slept. Some of it could be attributed to grieving for her father. The rest fell squarely on Diego's shoulders.

The electronic buzzer sounded loud above background music from wall-speakers, and Cassandra glanced up from her work to see a familiar figure holding twin food bags on the other side of the door.

Sally from the café near by with their lunch order.

'Want to take those sandwiches, or shall I?' Cassandra queried, only to see Glen in the throes of heating fine metal. 'OK, I'll get them.'

She laid down her tools, then moved towards the door, released the security lock and reached for the latch.

At that moment all hell let loose.

She had a fleeting glimpse of Sally's terrified expression, caught a blur of sudden movement as Sally catapulted into the workroom, followed by a man whose facial features were obscured by a woollen ski-mask.

A nightmare began to unfold as he whipped out a vicious-looking knife and brandished it.

The drill in such circumstances was clear. Do what you're told…and don't play the hero.

A knife wasn't a gun. She had self-defence training. Could she risk attempting to disarm him?

'Don't even think about it.' The harsh directive chilled her blood as he pulled out a hand gun and brandished it. In one swift movement he hooked an arm round her shoulders and hauled her back against him, then he pressed the tip of the knife to her throat.

Calm, she had to remain calm. Not easy with a

gun in close proximity, not to mention the threat of a knife.

At the edge of her peripheral vision she glimpsed Glen making a surreptitious move with his foot to the panic button at floor level. An action that would send an electronic alert to the supervisor's pager, the security firm and the local police station.

Had the intruder seen it? She could only pray not.

'Empty the vault.' The demand held a guttural quality, and she saw Glen lift his hands in a helpless gesture.

'I don't know the combination.'

He was buying time, and the intruder knew it.

'You think I'm a fool?' the intruder demanded viciously, tightening his hold on Cassandra's shoulders. 'Open it *now*, or I'll use this knife.'

She felt the tip of it slide across the base of her throat, the sting of her flesh accompanied by the warm trickle of blood.

Glen didn't hesitate. He crossed to the vault, keyed in a series of digits, then pulled open the door.

'Put everything into a bag. *Go!*'

Glen complied, moving as slowly as he dared.

'You want me to hurt her bad?'

The knife pressed hard, and Cassandra gasped at the pain.

'I'm being as quick as I can.' And he was, withdrawing trays, tossing the contents into a bag. 'That's all of it.'

'Give it to me!' He released her, and backed towards the workshop door.

She saw what he could not, and she deliberately kept her expression blank as two armed security guards positioned themselves each side of the outer door.

One well-aimed kick, the element of surprise, that was all it would take to disarm the intruder and provide the essential few seconds' confusion to give the guards their opportunity to burst in and take him down.

She went into calculated action, so fast it was over in seconds as her foot connected with his wrist and the gun went flying.

A stream of obscenities rent the air as he lunged for her, and she barely registered the door crashing open, or the security guards' presence as he swung her in against him.

Oh, God. The pressure against her ribs was excruciating, and she had difficulty breathing.

Sally began to cry quietly.

'Let her go.' One of the security guards made it a statement, not a plea, and earned a scathing glare.

'Are you crazy? She's going to be my ticket out of here!'

'Put down the knife.'

'Not in this lifetime, pal.' His snarl was low, primal, and frightening.

What began as a robbery had now become a hostage situation.

Then Cassandra heard it…the distant sound of a siren, the noise increasing in velocity, followed by the diminishing sonorous wail as the engine cut.

Seconds later the phone rang.

'Pick it up!'

The guard's movements were careful as he obeyed, listened, spoke, then he held out the receiver to her captor. 'It's for you.'

'Tell the man I want clear passage out of here and a fifteen-minute start. That's the deal.'

They wouldn't buy it. At least, not without resorting to any one of several psychological ploys in an attempt at negotiation.

The scene was too close to a movie script. Worse, the man holding her was desperate and wouldn't hesitate to hurt her.

Did your life flash before your eyes in a moment of extreme crisis? Cassandra pictured her mother, father. Cameron was there. *Diego.* Oh, hell, why Diego?

She didn't have a future with Diego. Dammit, she might not have a future at all!

'I want all of you out. *Now!*' He was incandescent with rage, and she consciously held her breath.

The guards, Sally and Glen filed out quietly, the door closed, leaving only Cassandra and the madman in the workshop.

'We're going to take a ride together, you and me.' His voice was close to her ear. 'If you're very good,

I just might let you go when we've put in some distance from here.'

Sure. And the sun shone bright at midnight in the Alaskan winter-time.

His hand closed over her breast, and squeezed. 'Or maybe you and me could shack up together awhile, have some fun.'

'In your dreams.'

He pinched her, hard, then thrust her roughly against a work-bench. 'Pick up that damned phone, and tell those bastards to get their act together.'

She could hardly believe they'd let him walk out of here alone. The gems in the vault were worth a small fortune. And there was the matter of her life.

Her hand stung, and she saw blood seeping from a deep cut as she lifted the receiver.

'Stay calm. Do what he says. We've set up road blocks. He can't get far.' The masculine voice was quiet, steady. As if he controlled a hostage situation on a weekly basis. Maybe he did, she thought wildly.

'They make a wrong move, and you're history, y'hear?'

What happened next was a nightmare of action, noise, fear in a kaleidoscope of motion as she was forced to carry the bag of gems, then used as a human shield as her captor hustled her towards his waiting car.

Would they try to take him out? Shoot, or hold their fire?

In those few terrifying seconds out in the open she consciously prepared herself for anything, and it wasn't until he shoved her across the driver's seat and climbed in almost on top of her that she realised he was about to make good his escape.

Taking her with him.

He fired the ignition and surged forward, wheels screeching as he took off at a frightening speed.

Cassandra automatically reached for the dashboard, not that it afforded her any purchase, and heard his maniacal laughter as he swerved in and out of traffic, then he took a hard turn left, only to scream with rage as he saw the road block up front.

She barely had a second to gauge his next move when he swung the car round and roared back down the road to crash through a hastily set-up road block.

The car bounced off another vehicle with a sickening thud of grinding metal before careening off down the road. Car horns blasted, brakes screamed.

Cassandra saw impending disaster a few seconds ahead of contact, and she acted entirely on impulse, throwing open the passenger door and leaping out an instant before the car hit.

There was a moment of searing pain as her body hit the asphalt, a conscious feeling of movement, then nothing.

Cassandra was dreaming. Her body felt strangely weightless, and at some stage she seemed to drift towards consciousness, only to retreat into a non-intrusive comfort zone.

There were voices, indistinguishable at first, then invasive as she came fully awake.

White walls, bustling movement, the faint smell of antiseptic…and a uniformed nurse hovering close checking her vital signs.

Hospital.

She became aware of an intravenous drip, bandages on one arm…and the dull ache of medicated pain. Her head, shoulder, hip.

'Good. You're awake.'

And alive. Somehow that fact held significance!

The nurse spared Cassandra a steady look. 'Multiple contusions, grazed skin, superficial knife wounds. Concussion.'

No fractures, no broken bones. That had to be a plus!

'We have you on pain relief. Doctor will be in soon. Meantime, you have a visitor.' Someone who had descended on the hospital within minutes of the patient being admitted, the nurse acknowledged silently. Insistently demanding the best specialists be summoned, and the patient allocated a private suite. Each attempt to compromise had been met with a steely glare.

'A visitor?'

'If you don't feel up to it, I can have him wait.' It wouldn't hurt to have him cool his heels a little longer. And if he dared upset the patient, she'd have his guts for garters.

Who knew she was here? It was probably a police officer needing her statement.

'It's OK.'

'Five minutes,' the nurse stipulated, and left the suite.

No sooner had she swept through the door, than it swung back and Diego entered. A tall, dark force whose presence seemed to fill the room.

Her surprised expression brought a faint smile to his lips, one that didn't reach his eyes as he advanced towards the bed.

'No *hello*?' He lowered his head and brushed his lips to her cheek.

Not even being pumped up with painkillers stilled the fluttering inside her stomach, nor did it prevent her quickening pulse. 'I'm temporarily speechless.'

'That I should come visit?' He kept his voice light, and wondered if she had any idea what he'd been through in the past few hours. Anger…hell, no, *rage* on being informed what had happened. And fear. Unadulterated fear he could have lost her.

He was still fighting both emotions, controlling them by sheer force of will. Her captor would pay…and pay dearly for putting this woman's life at risk.

'No one could stop me,' Diego drawled, his voice a mix of steel and silk.

Cassandra looked at him with unblinking solemnity. 'Who would dare?' His power was a given. His use of it, unequivocal.

His expression softened, and his eyes warmed a little. 'How are you, *querida*?'

The quietly voiced endearment almost brought her undone. 'As comfortable as can be expected.'

He lifted a hand and trailed gentle fingers along the edge of her jaw. 'Is there anything you need?'

You. Except he wasn't hers to have. 'When can I get out of here?'

The pad of his thumb traced the lower curve of her mouth. 'A day or two.'

She had to ask. 'My abductor?'

Diego's features became a hard mask. 'Arrested and behind bars.'

So there was justice, after all.

The door opened and the nurse returned. 'I must ask you to leave. The patient needs to rest.'

For a moment Cassandra thought he was going to refuse, then he moved in close, lowered his head and covered her mouth with his own.

It was a gentle kiss, and his tongue slid in to tangle briefly with hers. Electrifying seconds that sent a rush of blood to her head. Then he straightened, touched a light finger to her cheek, and vacated the suite.

Flowers arrived late afternoon. A bouquet from the workshop staff, and three dozen red roses with *'Diego'* scrawled in black ink on the attached card, together with a special-delivery package from one of the élite lingerie boutiques.

'Definitely *ah-hh* time,' an attentive nurse declared as Cassandra revealed two exquisite nightgowns and a matching robe. There were also essential toiletries—Chanel. He was nothing if not observant.

Cassandra ate little, endured a short visit from the police, gave a detailed account covering events during and after the robbery.

Then she slept, and she was unaware of Diego's presence in the room as he stood observing her features in repose.

So small, such a petite frame. Porcelain skin, and a mouth to die for.

He wanted to gather her up and take her home. To share his bed and hold her through the night. Just so he could. To protect, and ensure no one ever got close enough to hurt her again.

He, Diego del Santo, who'd bedded any number of women in his lifetime, now only wanted to bed one.

A slip of a thing, whose beautiful blue eyes had captivated him from the start. Without any effort at all she'd slipped beneath his skin and stolen his heart.

Was she aware of the effect she had on him?

The question was what he intended to do about it.

*   *   *

Cassandra woke early, accepted the nursing ritual and took a supervised shower. This morning the intravenous drip would be removed, and she wanted out of here.

The specialist was less than enthusiastic. 'I'd prefer you remained under observation for another twenty-four hours.'

'Prefer, but it's not essential?'

'Do you live alone?'

Tricky. 'Not exactly.' A resident cat didn't count. But she had the phone, her cellphone, and a caring neighbour.

He checked her vital signs, perused her chart. 'Let's effect a compromise. I'll check on you this afternoon with a view to possible release.' He gave her a piercing look. 'You have someone to collect and drive you home?'

She'd take a cab.

Which she did, arriving at her apartment just after six that evening. The manager produced a spare key and there was a sense of relief in being *home*.

The cat greeted her with a plaintive protest, and she fed her, put down fresh water, then made herself a cup of tea.

The *ouch* factor was very much in evidence, and she swallowed another two painkillers.

A nice quiet evening viewing television followed by an early night. By Monday she should be able to return to work.

Cassandra settled comfortably on the sofa, and

smiled as the cat jumped onto her lap. She surfed the television channels, selected a half-hour comedy and prepared to relax.

The insistent ring of the intercom buzzer was an unwelcome intrusion, and she transferred the cat, then moved to check the security screen.

Diego.

She picked up the in-house phone. 'I'm fine, and I'm about to go to bed.'

'Release the door.' His voice was deceptively mild.

'I'm too tired for visitors.'

'You want for me to get the manager and explain you left hospital under false pretences?'

'I already spoke to him. He gave me a spare key.'

'Cassandra—'

'Leave me alone. Please,' she added, then she re-placed the receiver and moved back to take up her position on the sofa.

The cat had just re-settled itself on her lap when her doorbell rang. Her neighbour?

The manager, she determined through the peep-hole, with Diego at his side.

She unlocked and opened the door. The manager looked almost contrite. 'Your—er—friend expressed concern about your welfare.'

'As you can see, I'm fine.' If she discounted the pain factor.

Diego turned towards the man at his side. 'I'll take it from here.'

He looked momentarily nonplussed. 'Cassandra?'

What could she say? 'It's OK.'

Seconds later she closed the door and turned to face the man who'd managed to turn her life upside-down. 'Just what do you think you're doing?'

He was silent for a fraction too long, and there was something very controlled in his manner. 'You want me to pack a bag, or will you?'

'I beg your pardon?'

'You heard,' Diego said calmly. 'You get to come with me, or I sleep here.' His gaze lanced hers, and there was no mercy in the silkiness of his voice. 'Choose, Cassandra.'

'I don't want you here.' It was a cry from the heart, and her breath hitched at the pain from her ribs.

Diego's eyes went dark, and a muscle bunched at his jaw. Without a word he turned and made for her bedroom.

'You can't do this!' Dammit, he was several steps ahead of her.

'Watch me.'

'Diego…' She faltered to a halt at the sight of him opening drawers and tossing contents into a holdall before crossing to her walk-in wardrobe, where he chose clothes at random. From there he moved into the *en suite* and swept items into a toiletry pouch.

'OK, let's go.'

'I'm not going anywhere with you!'

'Yes, you are. On your feet, or I get to carry you.'

He waited a beat. 'On your feet is the better option.'

Cassandra wanted to hit him...*hard*. 'Just who in hell do you think you are?' she demanded furiously.

Diego sought control, and found it. 'You need to rest, recuperate. I intend to see that you do.'

'I can look after myself.'

'Sure you can.' He closed the zip fastener on the holdall and caught the straps in one hand. 'Next week.'

His gaze seared hers in open challenge. 'Until then, I get to call the shots.'

'And if I refuse?'

'I carry you out of here.'

There was no doubt he meant every word. Dignity was the key, and she observed it in silence as she followed him out into the lobby, then rode the lift down to the entrance foyer.

The Aston Martin was parked immediately outside, and she slid into the passenger seat, then watched as he crossed round to the driver's side.

Minutes later they joined the flow of traffic, traversing the relatively short distance to his Point Piper home.

Cassandra barely held her temper. He was the most impossible man she'd ever had the misfortune to meet. Dictatorial, indomitable, omnipotent.

She could think of several more descriptions, none of which were ladylike.

Diego swept the car along the driveway, activated the modem controlling the garage doors, then eased to a halt and switched off the engine.

Cassandra heard the dull click as the doors closed and made no attempt to exit the car.

'How long do you intend to sulk?'

She threw him a fulminating glare. 'I don't *sulk*.' She drew in a deep breath, and winced. 'I simply have nothing to say to you.'

Whereas he had a lot to say to her about taking risks and being a hero. Dammit, did she have any idea what the outcome could have been?

His blood ran cold just thinking about it.

However, it would have to wait. If she felt anywhere near as fragile as she looked, the only thing she needed right now was some tender loving care.

Diego slid out from behind the wheel and reached for her holdall, then he crossed round to open the passenger door. 'Let's take this inside.' He reached in and released her safety belt.

'I'd prefer to go home.'

'We've already done this.'

So they had, but she was in a perverse mood and uninclined to comply.

'Stubborn.' He slid one arm beneath her knees and lifted her out from the car, then he bent down, caught up the holdall, used one hip to close the car door, and strode through to the foyer.

'I hate you,' Cassandra said fiercely.

'It's a healthy emotion.'

'Put me down.'

He began ascending the stairs. 'Soon.'

'If you intend taking me to bed, I'll *hit* you.'

They gained the gallery, and reached the master suite seconds later, where he lowered her gently down onto her feet. With deft movements he turned back the covers and built up a nest of pillows.

'Get into bed. I'll bring you a cup of tea.'

'I don't need you to play nursemaid.'

Diego loosened his tie and discarded his jacket, and threw both over a nearby chair. 'It's here with me, or the hospital.'

'You're giving me a choice?'

He undid the top few buttons of his shirt. 'I made the choice for you.' He walked to the door, then paused as he turned to face her. 'If you're not in bed when I come back, I'll put you there.'

'Fat chance.' Empty retaliatory words that gave her a degree of satisfaction.

She spared a glance at the bed, and the comfort it offered was sufficient for her to snag a nightshirt and toiletries from her holdall, then retreat with them into the *en suite*.

Every movement hurt, her body ached, and she began to wonder at her wisdom in leaving hospital too soon.

Minutes later she emerged into the bedroom and slid carefully beneath the covers. It would be so easy just to close her eyes and drift off to sleep.

Diego re-entered the room, tray in hand, and quietly closed the door behind him. The snack and hot tea could wait. He could wait.

Just the sight of her lying in repose against the nest of pillows was enough to stop the breath in his throat and send his heart thudding to a faster beat.

He should dim the lights, exit the room quietly and let her sleep.

He did the first, laid down the tray, then settled his lengthy frame into a chair. There was a sense of satisfaction in watching over her.

Here was where she belonged. Where he wanted her to stay.

Diego sat there for a long time, alert to her faintest move, the slightest murmur of pain. In the depth of night he extracted two painkillers, part-filled a glass with water, then had her swallow both.

Only when she slipped effortlessly back to sleep did he discard his clothes and slide carefully in beneath the bedcovers to lay awake until the early pre-dawn hours.

CHAPTER NINE

CASSANDRA drifted through the veils of sleep into wakefulness, aware from the room's shadowed light that night had become morning. Early morning, unless she was mistaken.

Her body tuned into numerous bruises and made her painfully aware that any sudden movement on her part was not going to be a good idea.

The bed, this room…they weren't her own. Then she remembered…and wished she hadn't.

She turned her head slowly and encountered Diego's dark gaze. He lay on his side, facing her, his body indolently at ease as he appraised her features.

An improvement on last night, he perceived, lifting a hand to brush a swathe of hair back from her cheek.

His eyes narrowed at the thin line inches long at the base of her throat. It would heal, and after a while the scar would fade.

'Want to talk about it?'

'A verbal post-mortem?' She tried for flippancy, and failed miserably. 'The facts are in the official report.'

Facts he'd read, assimilated, and dealt with. 'You

didn't follow the book.' He still went cold at the thought of what could have happened.

'Concern for my welfare, Diego?'

'That surprises you?'

It seeded a germ of hope. She attempted a light shrug, and didn't quite pull it off. 'Banking, gem merchants and jewellers are high-risk industries for robbery.'

So they were. But employees were drilled to respond passively, not attack or act with aggression.

'You scared the hell out of me.' He traced the outline of her mouth with a gentle finger. 'Next time don't be a hero, hmm?'

Cassandra didn't answer. No one in their right mind wanted a *next time*.

'What would you have done in a similar situation?'

Diego's eyes narrowed. He'd known the streets in his teens, lived on them for a while, worked them. Taken risks that brought him too close to the law, but never close enough to be caught. He'd carried a knife, but never a gun, studied and practised oriental techniques of combat and self-defence. Techniques that could kill a man with a well-aimed blow from the hand or foot.

In answer to her question, he would have judged the odds and taken a calculated risk. As she had done.

'If you dare tell me it's OK for a man, but not a

woman,' Cassandra said with quiet vehemence, 'I'll have to hit you.'

His eyes darkened and assumed a musing gleam. 'Now, that could prove interesting.'

She could only win if he allowed her to, she perceived, aware there were few, if any, capable of besting him in any arena.

There was much more beneath the surface than he permitted anyone to see. No one, not even the most diligent member of the media, had uncovered much of his past. It made her wonder if the shadows shielded something that didn't bear close scrutiny…and what there had been to mould him into the person he'd become.

'Hungry?'

For food or you? *Both*, she could have said and almost did. Except the former had priority, and was a much safer option than the latter.

Besides, she retained too vivid a memory of what they'd shared together in this bed.

'Shower, then breakfast.' Decisive words followed by smooth action as she slipped out of bed and crossed to the *en suite*.

Cassandra set the water temperature to warm, then she stepped into the glass and marble stall, caught up the shampoo and began with her hair.

There was a need to thoroughly cleanse her skin of her abductor's touch. She hated the memory of his hands, his almost manic expression, and the sound of his voice. It could have been worse, much worse, and she trembled at the thought. Delayed re-action, she determined, and vigorously massaged shampoo into her scalp.

'Let me help you with that.'

She stilled, locked into speechless immobility for a few electric-filled seconds, then she released the pent-up breath she'd unconsciously held. 'I can manage.'

'I don't doubt it,' Diego drawled, as he began a series of slow, soothing, circular movements.

His gaze narrowed as he took in her bruised rib-cage, the deep bluish marks on her arms. He wanted to touch his mouth to each one, and he would... soon. But for now he was content to simply care for her.

Dear heaven, Cassandra breathed silently. To stand here like this was sheer bliss... magical. She closed her eyes and let the strength of his fingers ease the tension from her scalp, the base of her neck, then work out the kinks at her shoulders.

He had the touch, the skill to render her body boneless, and an appreciative sound sighed from her lips as he caught up the soap and began smoothing it gently over the surface of her skin.

When he was done, he caught her close and cra-dled her slender frame against his own, then nuzzled the curve at her neck.

Diego felt her body tremble, and he trailed his mouth to hers in a gentle exploration that brought warm tears to her eyes.

Did he see them, taste them? she wondered, wanting only to wrap her arms round him and sink in. The temptation was so great, it took all her strength to resist deepening the kiss.

With considerable reluctance she dragged her mouth from his and rested her cheek against his chest.

It felt good, so good to be here with him like this. To take the comfort he offered, savour it and feel secure.

Cassandra felt him shift slightly, and the cascading water stilled.

'Food, hmm?' He slid open the door, snatched a towel and began rubbing the moisture from her body before tending to his own.

It took scant minutes to utilise toiletries and clean her teeth before she escaped into the bedroom, where she retrieved jeans and a loose shirt from her bag, then, dressed, she caught up a brush and restored order to her hair.

Diego emerged as she applied pins to secure its length, and her gaze strayed to his reflected image, mesmerised by the smooth flex of sinew and muscle as he donned black jeans and a polo shirt.

She tamped down the warmth flooding her veins, the core of need spiralling deep inside. Crazy, she acknowledged. She was merely susceptible to circumstance…and knew she lied.

He turned slightly and his gaze locked with hers. For a brief moment everything else faded from the periphery of her vision, and there was only the man and a heightened degree of electric tension in the room.

It felt as if her soul was being fused with his, like twin halves accepting recognition and magnetically drawn to become one entity.

Mesmeric, primitive, incandescent.

She forgot to breathe, and she stood still, like an image caught frozen in time and captured on celluloid.

Then the spell broke, and she was the first to move, thrusting her hands into the pockets of her jeans as she turned towards the door.

Had Diego felt it, too? Or was she merely being fanciful?

Coffee. She needed it hot, strong, black and sweet.

Cassandra took the stairs and made her way towards the kitchen, aware Diego followed only a step behind her.

'Go sit down on the terrace. I'll fix breakfast.'

Soon the aroma of freshly made coffee permeated the air, the contents in the skillet sizzled, and minutes later he placed two plates onto the table.

The morning sun held the promise of warmth, the air was still, and the view out over the infinity pool to the harbour provided a sense of tranquillity.

Cassandra ate well, much to her surprise. She hadn't expected to do the meal justice, and she pushed her empty plate to one side with a sense of disbelief.

'More coffee?' It was a token query as Diego re-filled her cup, then his own.

She felt at peace, calm after the previous afternoon's excitement.

'I'll call a cab.'

His expression remained unchanged, but there was a sense of something dangerous hovering beneath the surface. 'To go where?'

His tone was deceptively mild…too mild, she perceived. 'My apartment.' Where else?

He replaced his empty cup down onto its saucer with care. 'No.'

'What do you mean…*no*?'

'It's a simple word,' Diego drawled. 'One not difficult to understand.'

She looked at him carefully. 'I don't want to fight with you.'

'Wise choice.'

'But—'

'There has to be a *but*?'

It was time to take a deep breath…except her ribs hurt too much, and she had to be content with *shallow*. 'Thank you for—' She paused fractionally. For what? Taking care of her, bringing her here…caring. Oh, hell, she had to keep it together! 'Looking after me,' she concluded. 'It was very kind.'

He was silent for a few measurable seconds, and his eyes narrowed, masking a hardness that was at variance with the softness of his voice. 'Are you done?'

'Yes.' She waited a beat. 'For now.'

'I'm relieved to hear it.'

He was something else. All hard, muscular planes, and leashed strength as he leaned back in his chair, looking as if he owned the world…and her.

Total power, she accorded silently, and was determined not to be swayed by his sense of purpose.

Cassandra discarded her coffee and rose to her feet, then began stacking empty plates onto a tray, only to have it taken from her hands.

Without a further word she moved from the room and made her way upstairs.

It didn't take much to scoop her belongings into the holdall Diego had thrust them in the previous evening, and minutes later she picked up the bedroom extension, punched in the digits for a cab company, and was in the process of giving instructions when Diego entered the room.

Without a word he crossed to where she stood and cut the connection.

An action which sparked indignant anger as she turned to face him. 'How *dare* you?'

'Easily.'

'You have no right—'

He held up a hand. 'Last night you discharged yourself from hospital against medical advice. Your brother is in Melbourne, and unless I'm mistaken he's unaware of yesterday's escapade. You live alone.' His eyes were dark and held a latent anger that most would shrink from. 'Want me to go on?'

'I don't need a self-appointed guardian.'

'Like it or not, you've got one...for another twenty-four hours at least.'

Her chin tilted. 'You can't force me to stay.'

'It's here, or hospital readmission,' Diego said succinctly. 'Choose.'

She considered punching him, then discarded the idea on the grounds it would inevitably hurt her more than it would him. 'You're a dictatorial tyrant,' she said at last.

'I've been called worse.'

He wasn't going to budge. She could see it in his stance, the muscle bunching at his jaw.

'Who said you get to make the rules?' It was a cry from the heart, rendered in anger.

He didn't answer. He didn't need to.

'I need to feed my cat.' She threw one hand in the air to emphasise the point, then winced as pain shot through her body. 'Dammit.'

Diego swung between an inclination to shake or kiss her, considered the former followed by the latter, then went with rationale. 'So, we'll go feed him.'

'She,' Cassandra corrected. 'The cat's a *she*.'

He collected his keys and moved towards the door, then paused, turning slightly to look at her when she hadn't shifted position. 'You need to think about it?'

She wanted to throw something at him, and would have if there had been something close at hand. Instead she opted for capitulation…reluctantly.

Silence won over recrimination during the short drive to her apartment building, and she cast Diego a hard glance as he slid from behind the wheel.

'You don't have to come up with me.' What did he think she might do? Lock herself in? A speculative gleam lit her eyes…now, there was a thought!

He didn't answer as he joined her at the security area immediately adjacent to the entrance, and she restrained from uttering an audible sigh as he walked at her side to the bank of lifts.

A deeply wounded *miaow* greeted her the moment she unlocked her apartment door, and the cat butted its head against her leg in welcome.

Bite him, Cassandra silently instructed as Diego leant down and fondled the cat's ears.

The cat purred in affectionate response, and ignored her.

Great. Three years of food, a bed to sleep on and unconditional love…for all that I get ignored? There was no accounting for feline taste.

It took only minutes to put down food and fresh water, and Cassandra spared Diego a level look. 'I'm fine. Really.'

One eyebrow rose. 'So…go now and leave me alone?' He examined her features, assessing the pale cheeks, the dark blue eyes. 'We've done this already.'

So they had, but she felt akin to a runaway train that couldn't stop. 'I'm sure you have a social engagement lined up for this evening.' It was, after all, Saturday. 'I'd hate to be the reason you cancelled. Or cause problems with your latest—' she paused momentarily '—date.'

'Are you through?'

'I don't want to be with you.'

He didn't move, but she had the impression he shifted stance. How did he do that? Go from apparent relaxation mode to menacing alert?

'Afraid, Cassandra?'

Yes, she wanted to cry out. Not of you. Myself. For every resolve I make away from you disintegrates into nothing whenever you're near. And I can't, *won't* allow myself to fall to pieces over you.

Too late, a silent imp taunted. You're already an emotional wreck.

Every reason for her to walk away *now.* If only he would leave.

'Of yourself…or me?' Diego queried quietly.

Her chin tilted. 'Both.'

His mouth curved into a soft smile. 'Ah, honesty.' His gaze swept the room. 'If there's nothing else you need to do, we'll leave.'

Her lips parted in protest, only to close again as he pressed a finger against them.

'No argument, hmm?'

On reflection it was a restful day.

Within minutes of returning to Point Piper, Diego

excused himself on the pretext of work and entered the study, leaving Cassandra to amuse herself as she pleased.

She made a few calls from her cellphone, then she browsed through a few glossy magazines. Lunch was a light meal of chicken and salad eaten alfresco, and afterwards she slotted a DVD into the player and watched a movie.

Work took Diego's attention, leaving her with little option but to spend time alone. Restless, she ventured outdoors and wandered the grounds, admiring the garden.

Flowers were in bud, providing a colourful array in sculpted beds. Topiary clipped with expert precision, and a jacaranda tree in bloom, its fallen petals providing a carpet of lavender beneath spreading branches.

She reached the pool area, and she ascended the few terracotta-tiled steps to the terrace, crossed to a comfortable lounge setting beneath a shaded umbrella and sank into a seat.

The pool sparkled and shimmered beneath the sun's warmth, its infinity design providing the illusion its surface melded with the harbour beyond. Subtle shades of blue…pool, harbour, sky.

A sense of peace reigned as she took in the magnificent panoramic view. The city with its tall buildings of concrete and glass, the distinctive lines of the Opera House, the harbour bridge. Not to mention various craft skimming the waters and numerous mansions dotting the numerous coves.

Beautiful position, magnificent home.

And the man who owned it?

Cassandra closed her eyes against his powerful image. Four weeks ago he'd been a man she politely avoided.

Now... Dear heaven, she didn't want to think about *now*. Or what she was going to do about it. Hell, what *could* she do about it?

Loving someone didn't always end with happy-ever-after. And she wasn't the type to flit from one partner to another, enjoying the ride for however long it happened to last.

Tomorrow she'd return to her apartment, and her life as she knew it to be. Whenever her path crossed socially with Diego's, she'd greet him politely and move on. As she had during the past year.

Chance would be a fine thing, she alluded with unaccustomed cynicism. How could she do *polite* with a man with whom she'd shared every intimacy?

And fallen in love.

The to-the-ends-of-the-earth, the depth-of-the-soul kind.

Maybe she should take a leave of absence from the jewellery workshop and book a trip somewhere. A change of place, new faces.

Cassandra must have dozed, for she came awake at the sound of her name and a light touch on her shoulder.

'You fell asleep.' Diego didn't add that he'd kept watch over her for the past hour, reluctant to disturb her until the air cooled and the sun's warmth began to fade.

He was close, much too close. She could sense the clean smell of his clothes, the faint musky tones of his cologne. For a wild moment she had the over-whelming urge to reach up and pull his head down to hers, then angle her mouth in against his in a kiss that would rock them both.

Except such an action would lead to something she doubted she could handle...and walk away from.

His eyes darkened, almost as if he could read her thoughts, then he touched gentle fingers to her mouth and traced its curve.

'There's steak to go with salad. Go freshen up and we'll eat, hmm?'

Ten minutes later she sat opposite him, sampling succulent, melt-in-your-mouth beef fillet, together with crisp fresh salad and crunchy bread rolls.

'You can cook,' she complimented, and met his musing smile.

'That's an advantage?'

'For a man, definitely,' Cassandra conceded.

'Why, in this era when women maintain careers equal to those of men?'

'Do men think hearth and home, *food,* in quite the same way a woman does?' she countered.

'The man works to provide, while the woman nurtures?' He took a sip of wine. 'A delineation defining the sexes?'

'Equality in the workplace,' she broached with a tinge of humour. 'But outside of it, men and women are from two different planets.'

'And not meant to cohabit?'

'Physically,' she agreed. 'The emotional aspect needs work.'

'*Vive la difference,* hmm?'

It proved to be a leisurely meal, and afterwards they viewed a movie on DVD. When the credits rolled she rose to her feet and bade him a polite goodnight.

She couldn't, wouldn't slip into the bed she'd shared with him last night, she determined as she ascended the stairs to the upper level.

It took only minutes to collect her nightwear and toiletries and enter another bedroom. There were fresh sheets and blankets in the linen box at the foot of the bed, and she quickly made up the bed, undressed, then slid beneath the covers.

She was about to snap off the bedside light when the door opened and Diego entered the room.

'What are you doing here?'

'My question, I think,' he drawled as he crossed to the bed and threw back the covers. 'You want to walk, or do I get to carry you?'

'I'm not sleeping in your bed.'

'It's where you'll spend the night.'

Cassandra could feel the anger simmer beneath

the surface of her control. Soon, it would threaten to erupt. 'Sex as payment for you taking on the role of nursemaid?' She regretted the words the instant they left her lips.

'Would you care to run that by me again?' His voice sent icy shivers scudding down the length of her spine.

'Not really.'

Without a further word Diego turned and walked from the room, quietly closing the door behind him. An action that was far more effective than if he'd slammed it.

Dammit, what was the matter with her?

Subconsciously she knew the answer. Fear…on every level.

Ultimately, for losing something she'd never had…the love of a man. Not just any man. Diego del Santo.

Cassandra lay in the softly lit room, staring at the walls surrounding her, and faced the knowledge that life without him would amount to no life at all.

Her eyes ached with unshed tears, and she cursed herself for allowing her emotions free rein.

She had no idea how long it was before she fell into an uneasy sleep where dark figures chased her fleeing form.

At some stage she came sharply awake, immensely relieved to have escaped from a nightmarish dream. Until memory returned, and with it the knowledge she was alone in a bed in Diego's home...and why.

She closed her eyes in an effort to dispel his image, and failed miserably as she accorded herself all kinds of fool.

The admission didn't sit well, and after several long minutes she slid from the bed and crossed to the *en suite*.

There was a glass on the vanity top, and she part-filled it with water, then lifted the glass to her lips, only to have it slip from her fingers, hit the vanity top and fall to the tiled floor, where it shattered into countless shards.

It was an accident, and she cursed the stupid tears welling in her eyes as she sank down onto her haunches and collected the largest pieces of glass.

There was a box of tissues on the vanity top, and she reached for them, tore out several sheets and began gathering up the mess.

It became the catalyst that unleashed her withheld emotions, and the tears overflowed to run in warm rivulets down each cheek, clouding her vision.

'What the hell—?'

Cassandra was so intent on the task at hand she didn't hear Diego enter the room, and her fingers shook at the sound of his voice.

'I dropped a glass.' As if it wasn't self-explanatory.

He took one look at her attempt to gather the shards together, and the breath locked in his throat.

'Don't move.' The instruction was terse. 'I'll be back in a minute.'

He made it in three, and that was only because he had to discard one broom cupboard and search in another for a brush and pan.

In one fluid movement he lifted her high and lowered her down onto the bedroom carpet, then he completed the clean-up with deft efficiency.

Cassandra could only stand and watch, mesmerised by the sight of him in hastily pulled-on jeans, the breadth of his shoulders and the flex of muscle and sinew.

He made her ache in places where she had little or no control, and she turned away, wanting only for him to leave before she lost what was left of her composure.

'Use one of the other bathrooms until morning just in case there are any splinters I might have missed.'

She had difficulty summoning her voice. 'Thanks.' She made a helpless gesture with one hand. 'I'm sorry the noise disturbed you.'

Did she have any idea how appealing she looked? Bare legs, a cotton nightshirt with a hem that reached mid-thigh, and her hair loose and tousled?

No other woman had affected him quite the way she did. He wanted to reach beneath the nightshirt, fasten his hands on warm flesh and skim them over her skin. Touch, and be touched in return in a prelude that could only have one end.

'Are you OK?'

How did she answer that? She'd never be *OK* where he was concerned. 'I'm fine.' An automatic response, and one that took first prize in the fabrication stakes.

'I'll get rid of this.'

The pan, brush and broken glass. She nodded, aware he crossed to the door, and she registered the moment he left the room.

She should get into bed, douse the light and try to get some sleep. Instead she sank down onto the edge of the mattress and buried her head in her hands.

Reaction could be a fickle thing, and she let the tears fall. Silently, wondering if their release would ease the heartache made worse by having crossed verbal swords with the one man who'd come to mean so much to her in such a short time.

It was crazy to swing like a pendulum between one emotion and another. The sooner she returned to her apartment and moved on with her life, the better.

She wanted what she had before Diego del Santo tore her equilibrium to shreds and scattered her emotional heart every which way.

Oh, *dammit*, why did love have to hurt so much?

With a sense of frustration she rubbed her cheeks and smoothed the hair back from her face. It was then she saw Diego's tall frame in the open doorway.

If there was anything that undid a man, Diego acknowledged, it was a woman's tears. He'd witnessed many in his time. Some reflecting genuine grief; others merely a manipulative act.

None had the effect on him to quite the degree as evidence of this woman's distress did.

There were occasions when words healed, but now wasn't the time.

In silence he crossed the room and gathered her into his arms, stilling her protest by the simple expediency of placing the palm of one hand over her mouth.

It took a matter of seconds to reach the master suite, and he released her carefully down onto her feet.

Without a word he skimmed the nightshirt over her head and tossed it onto the carpet, then followed it with his jeans.

'What do you think you're doing?' As a protest it failed, utterly.

His eyes were dark, so dark she thought she might drown in them, as he captured her arms and slid his hands up to cup her face.

'This is the one place where everything between us makes sense,' he drawled as his head lowered down to hers.

She felt the warmth of his breath a second before his mouth took possession of hers in a kiss that liquefied her bones.

A faint moan rose and died in her throat as he

took her deep, so deep she lost track of where and who she was as emotion ruled, transcending anything they'd previously shared.

Somehow they were no longer standing, and she gasped as Diego's mouth left hers and began a slow descent, savouring the sensitive hollow at the edge of her neck before trailing a path over the line at the base of her throat where her captor had pierced her skin with the tip of his knife.

With the utmost care Diego caressed each bruise, as if to erase the uncaring brutality of the man who'd inflicted them.

The surface of her skin became highly sensitised, and her pulse raced to a quickened beat, thudding in unison with his own. She could feel it beneath her touch, the slide of her fingers.

What followed became a leisurely, sweet loving, so incredibly tender Cassandra was unable to prevent the warm trickle of tears, and when at last he entered her she cried out, exulting in the feel of him as warm, moist tissues expanded to accept his length.

Sensation spiralled to new heights, and she wrapped her legs around his waist, urging him deep, thrilling to each thrust as he slowly withdrew, only to plunge again and again in the rhythm of two lovers in perfect unison in their ascent to the brink of ecstasy.

Diego held her there, teetering on the edge, before

tipping them both over in a sensual free-fall that left them slick with sweat and gasping for breath.

The aftermath became a gentle play of the senses, with the soft trail of fingertips, the light touch of lips.

CHAPTER TEN

CASSANDRA stirred, and gradually became aware she wasn't alone in the bed. For her head lay pillowed against Diego's chest, a male leg rested across her own, and his arms loosely circled her body as he held her close.

Diego sensed the quickened heartbeat, the change in her breathing, and brushed his lips to her hair. Tousled silk, he mused, inhaling its fresh, clean smell. A man could take immense pleasure from waking each morning with a warm, willing woman in his arms.

Not just any woman...*this* woman.

'You're awake.'

She heard his quiet drawl, *felt* the sound of it against her cheek, and offered a lazily voiced affirmative.

He trailed the tips of his fingers down the length of her spine, shaped the firm globe of her buttock, then he traced a path over her hip, settled briefly in the curve of her waist before shifting to her breast.

There was a part of her that knew she should protest. To slip so easily into intimacy meant she accepted the current situation...and she didn't.

Dear heaven. She bit back a gasp as he eased her

172

gently onto her back, then lowered his mouth to suckle at one tender peak.

Seconds later the breath hissed between her teeth as his hand trailed to the soft curls at the apex of her thighs and began a teasing exploration.

She went up and over, then groaned out loud as another orgasmic wave chased the first with an intensity that took hold of her emotions and spun them out of control.

His arousal was a potent force, and just as she thought she'd scaled the heights he nudged her thighs apart, slid in, and took her higher than she'd ever been before, matching her climax with his own in a tumultuous fusion of the senses.

It took a while for their breathing to settle into its former rhythm, and they lay entwined together, spent as only two people could be in the aftermath of very good sex.

Make that incredible, off-the-planet sex, Cassandra amended as she closed her eyes and indulged her mind and body in an emotional replay.

It had, she mused indolently, been all about her pleasure. Soon, she'd seek to even the scales a little.

And she did, later, taking delight in testing his control…and breaking it.

Enjoy, Cassandra bade silently. For within a few hours she'd return to her apartment and a life from which Diego would fade.

Later, much later they rose from the bed, shared a shower, then, dressed, they descended the stairs to the kitchen for a meal that was neither breakfast nor lunch but a combination of both.

Diego's cellphone buzzed as they lingered over coffee, and he checked the caller ID, then rose to his feet.

'I'll have to take this.'

Cassandra lifted a hand, silently indicating he should do so, and she watched as he crossed the terrace.

French, she registered, barely discerning a word or two…and wondered how many languages he spoke.

Business, she determined, and let her gaze drift across the pool to the harbour beyond.

'I have to meet with two business colleagues. Their scheduled stopover was cancelled and they took an earlier flight,' Diego relayed as he returned to the table. 'I'll be an hour or two.' He drained the rest of his coffee, then leant down and took brief, hard possession of her mouth. 'We need to talk.' His lips caressed hers with a soothing touch.

She wasn't capable of saying a word, and he uttered a husky imprecation.

'Cassandra—'

The insistent sound of his cellphone brought forth a harsh expletive, and she saw the flex of muscle at his jaw as he sought civility. 'Dammit.' He raked fingers through his hair.

'It's OK.'

His eyes darkened. It was far from OK. Yet delegation was out of the question. There were only two associates capable of handling the current negotiations, and neither were in the same state.

'I should be able to tie this up within an hour or two.'

'Go,' she managed quietly. 'They,' whoever *they* were, 'will be waiting for you.'

He shot her a piercing look, then turned and made his way through the house, collected his briefcase and keys and entered the garage.

Minutes later Cassandra stood to her feet, cleared the table, then dealt with dishes and tidied the kitchen.

Stay, or leave.

If she stayed, she'd be condoning an affair. And while she could live with that if mutual *love* was at its base, she found it untenable when the emotion was one-sided.

She wasn't an 'it's OK as long as it lasts' girl. Nor could she view hitching up with a man for whatever she'd gain from the relationship.

No contest, she decided sadly as she made her way upstairs.

It didn't take long to pack, or to pen a note which she propped against the side-table in the foyer. Then she crossed to the phone and called for a cab.

The cat greeted her with an indignant sound and a swishing tail. The message light on her answering machine blinked, and she organised priorities by feeding the cat, then she tossed clothes into the

washing machine, fetched a cool drink, then she ran
the machine.

Siobhan…'Tying the knot in Rome next weekend. Need you there, darling, to hold my hand.'

Cameron…'Flying home Tuesday. Let's do dinner Wednesday, OK?'

Alicia…'Hope you're enjoying the ride. It won't
last.'

Cassandra didn't know whether to laugh or cry at
the latter. The ride, as Alicia called it, was over.

Keeping busy would help, and when the washing-
machine cycle finished she put the clean clothes into
the drier.

The contents of the refrigerator looked pathetic,
and she caught up her car keys. Milk, bread, fresh
fruit and salad headed her mental list, and she took
the lift down to the basement car park, then drove
to the nearest store.

There was a trendy café close by, and she ordered
a latte, picked up a magazine, and leafed through
the pages while she sipped her coffee.

It was almost five when she swept the car into the
bricked apron adjacent to the apartment building's
main entrance, automatically veering left to take the
descending slope into the basement car park.

It was then she saw a familiar car parked in the
visitors' area. As if there was any doubt, Diego's
tall frame leaning indolently against the Aston
Martin's rear panel merely confirmed it.

For a few heart-stopping seconds she forgot to

breathe, then she eased her car towards the security gate, retrieved her ID card and inserted it with shaking fingers and drove down to her allotted space, killed the engine, then reached for the door-clasp…only to have the door swing open before she had a chance to release it.

She tilted her head to look at him, and almost wished she hadn't, for his features appeared carved from stone.

'What are you doing here?'

'Did you think I wouldn't come after you?'

She felt at a distinct disadvantage seated in the car. By comparison he seemed to tower over her, and if they were going to get into a heated argument she needed to even the stakes a little.

With careful movements she slid from behind the wheel, then closed and locked the door before turning to face him. 'I don't know what you're talking about.'

'Yes, you do.' His voice resembled pure silk, and she swallowed the sudden lump that rose in her throat.

'Why didn't you stay?'

'There was no reason to,' she managed. 'We don't owe each other a thing.'

'All obligations fulfilled,' Diego accorded with dangerous softness.

It almost killed her to say it. 'Yes.'

'No emotional involvement. Just good sex?'

She was breaking up, ready to shatter. 'What do

you want from me?' It was a cry from the heart that held a degree of angry desperation.

'I want you in my life.'

'For how long, Diego?' she demanded. 'Until either one of us wants it to end?' As it would. 'Nothing lasts forever, and lust is a poor bedfellow for love.'

A car swept close by and slid into an adjacent space. She recognised the driver as a fellow tenant, and she met his concerned glance.

'Everything OK, Cassandra?'

Diego hardly presented a complacent figure. She managed a reassuring smile. 'Yes.'

The tenant cast Diego a doubtful look, glimpsed a sense of purpose in those dark eyes, and chose to move on.

'Let's take this upstairs.'

If he touched her, she'd be lost. One thing would lead to another…

It was better to end it now. 'No.'

Diego barely resisted the temptation to shake her. 'Tell me what we share means nothing to you.'

She couldn't do it. Her eyes clouded, then darkened as she struggled to find something to say that wouldn't sound inane.

Some of the tension eased in his gut as he reached for her. He cupped her nape with one hand and drew her in against him with the other, then his mouth was on hers, moving like warm silk as he took possession.

When he lifted his head she could only look at him.

'You're a piece of work,' he accorded quietly. 'No woman has driven me as crazy as you have.' His lips curved into a warm smile. 'A year of being held at a distance, when you've politely declined every invitation I extended. I've had to be content with brief, well-bred conversations whenever we attended the same social functions.'

Cassandra recalled each and every one of those occasions. The edgy onset of nerves the instant his familiar frame came into view; a recognition on some deep emotional level she was afraid to explore, fearing if she entered his space she'd never survive leaving it.

'Marry me.'

Cassandra opened her mouth, then closed it again. 'What did you say?'

'Marry me.'

She could only look at him in shocked silence.

'Do you really want our children to learn their father proposed to their mother in a basement car park?' Diego queried gently.

This was a bad joke. 'You can't be serious.'

'As serious as it gets.'

'Diego—'

'I want to share the rest of your life,' he said gently. 'I want to be the father of your children and grow old with you.'

There could be no doubt he meant every word. It

was there in the depth of his dark eyes, the heartfelt warmth of his voice, his touch.

Joy began a radiating spiral as it sang through her veins, piercingly sweet and gloriously sensual.

A faint smile lifted the edges of his mouth as he gave the concrete cavern a sweeping glance. 'I'd planned on different surroundings from these.'

Cassandra's lips parted in a tremulously soft smile. 'I don't need soft music, dimmed lights, fine food or wine.'

Diego brushed his fingers along the edge of her jaw, tilting her chin a little as he caressed the curve of her lower lip with his thumb. 'Just the words, *querida*?'

She felt as if she was teetering on the edge of something wonderful. 'Only if you mean them.'

'You're the love I thought I'd never find,' he said gently. 'I want, *need* you. *You*,' he emphasised gently. 'For the rest of my life.'

For a moment she didn't seem capable of finding her voice. It overwhelmed her. *He* overwhelmed her. In an instinctive gesture she pressed her mouth against his palm.

'I didn't want to like you,' Cassandra said shakily. 'I especially didn't want to fall in love with you.' She'd fought him every inch of the way, hating him for forcing recognition their souls were twin halves of a whole.

'Because of my so-called dangerous past?' he queried with teasing amusement.

'It shaped and made you the man you've become.' Providing the tenacity, strength of will and integrity lacking in many men his equal.

He fastened his mouth on hers in a kiss that was so evocatively tender it melted her bones.

Minutes later Diego caught hold of her hand and began leading her towards the lift. 'We need to get out of here.' His smile held the heat of passion overlayed with a tinge of humour. 'Your place or mine?'

'You're letting me make the decision?'

He paused to take a brief, hard kiss, tangled his tongue with hers, and felt the breath catch in her throat. 'You have a sassy mouth.'

'That's a compliment?'

Seconds later the lift doors opened and they entered the cubicle. 'Foyer?' Diego queried as he indicated the panel. 'Or your apartment?'

'There's the cat—'

'Not the foyer.'

The lift began its ascent towards her floor. 'I need clothes,' Cassandra continued.

'The cat will adjust.'

'To what?'

'Her new home.'

She looked at him, and melted. 'I love you.'

'Love me, love my cat?' he quizzed with amusement.

'Uh-huh. She's with me.' The lift slid to a stop, and she preceded him into the lobby.

He took the keys from her hand and unlocked and entered the apartment, then he closed the door behind them.

'I take it that's a *yes*?'

Her expression sobered as she looked at him. The love was there, for her, only her. She doubted anyone had ever seen him so vulnerable, and it moved her more than anything he could have said.

'Yes,' she said simply.

He needed to show her just how much she meant to him…and he did, with such thoroughness the end of the day faded into night, and it was after midnight when they raided the fridge, made an omelette, toast, and washed them both down with coffee.

'Groceries!' Cassandra exclaimed in despair. 'I left them in my car.' She thought of spoiled milk and other comestibles, and shook her head.

'Do you have any specific plans over the next few weeks?' Diego queried idly. She looked adorable, sparkling eyes, warm skin, and gloriously tumbled hair. He reached out a hand and pushed an errant swathe back behind her ear.

'Any particular reason?'

His smile assumed musing indulgence. 'A wedding. Ours.'

There would come a day when nothing he did or said would surprise her…but she had a way to go before that happened.

'Something low-key, in deference to your father. Just family, a few close friends. If you have your heart set on a traditional ceremony, we can reaffirm our vows in a few months.'

'Weeks?' Cassandra reiterated with a sense of stunned amusement. 'I'm due in Rome this weekend for Siobhan's wedding—'

'Perfect. We'll fly in together, spend some time there—'

She put up a hand. 'Whoa! You're going too fast.'

'And arrive back in time to meet our marriage-application requirements,' he concluded.

'The honeymoon before the wedding?' She tried for humour, and didn't quite make it.

'You object?'

How could she, when all she wanted to do was be with him? 'You take my breath away,' she admitted shakily in an attempt to get her head around organising a wedding, travel plans for Rome. Then there was work…

He witnessed her emotional struggle, and sought to ease it. 'All it involves is a series of phone calls. Let me take care of it.'

CHAPTER ELEVEN

ROME was magical, with Siobhan's wedding to her Italian count a glamorous event with much love and rejoicing.

The week that followed became a special time as Diego indulged Cassandra in a tour of the city's galleries, the exclusive jewellery boutiques, with leisurely lunches in one trendy trattoria or another. At night they visited a theatre, or lingered over dinner.

And made love with a passion that was both evocatively sensual and intensely primitive.

They flew in to Sydney three days before their own wedding was scheduled to take place. Days which merged one into the other as Cassandra ran a final check with the dressmaker, the florist, caught up with Cameron, and organised the last remaining items from her apartment to Diego's home.

Sunday dawned bright and clear, and within hours the last-minute touches were being made by various people employed to ensure every detail represented perfection.

Gardeners put finishing touches to the grounds, and florists lined the gazebo with white orchids. An altar was set ready for the marriage celebrant, and the caterers moved into the kitchen.

Cameron arrived ahead of the guests, and Cassandra accepted his careful hug minutes before they were due to emerge onto the red-carpeted aisle that led to the gazebo.

'Nervous?'

'Just a little.'

'Don't be,' he reassured, and she offered a shaky smile as the music began.

Diego stood waiting for her at the altar, and Cassandra's heart skipped a beat as he turned to watch her walk towards him.

Everything faded, and there was only the man.

Tall, dark and attractive, resplendent in a superbly tailored suit. But it was his expression that held her entranced. There was warmth, caring…and passion evident. Qualities she knew he'd gift her for the rest of his life.

In an unprecedented gesture he moved forward and took her hand in his, raised it to his lips, then he led her the remaining few yards to the gazebo.

It was a simple ceremony, with a mix of conventional and personal vows. By mutual consent, they'd agreed to choose each other's wedding ring.

Jewellery design was her craft, and Cassandra had selected a wide gold band studded with a spaced line of diamonds. It was masculine, different, and one of her personal designs.

There had been a degree of subterfuge in Diego's choice, for the ring he slipped onto her finger was a feminine match of his.

'For what we've already shared, what we have now,' Diego said gently, adding a magnificent solitaire diamond ring together with a circle of diamonds representing eternity. 'The future.'

She wanted to cry and smile at the same time, and she did both, one after the other, then gave a choking laugh as Diego angled his mouth over hers in a kiss that held such a degree of sensual promise it was all she could do to hold back the tears.

It was later, much later when they were alone, that she took the time to thank him.

Instead of booking a hotel suite, they'd opted to remain at home. It seemed appropriate, somehow, to spend their wedding night in the bed where they'd first made love.

'You're welcome,' Diego said gently as she slid her arms high and pulled his head down to hers.

'I love you.' Emotion reduced her voice to a husky sound. 'I always will.'

He brushed his lips across her forehead, then trailed a path to the edge of her mouth, angled in and took his time. '*Mi amante, mi mujer,* my life.'

A deliciously wicked smile curved her lips. '*Gracias, mi esposo.*'

Diego gave a husky laugh, and uttered something incomprehensible to her in Spanish.

'Translate.'

He offered a devilish grin. 'I'll show you.'

And he did.

On the edge of sleep he curled her close and held her…aware one lifetime would not be enough.

LIVE THE EMOTION

Modern Romance™
...seduction and
passion guaranteed

Tender Romance™
...love affairs that
last a lifetime

Medical Romance™
...medical drama
on the pulse

Historical Romance™
...rich, vivid and
passionate

Sensual Romance™
...sassy, sexy and
seductive

Blaze Romance™
...the temperature's
rising

27 new titles every month.

Live the emotion

MILLS & BOON®

MB3

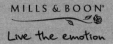

MILLS & BOON®

Live the emotion

Modern Romance™

MISTRESS FOR A MONTH *by Miranda Lee*

Rico Mandretti knows Renée Selensky despises him, and her history makes her as potent as poison. Then Fate delivers Rico an unbeatable hand: he wins a game of cards – and Renée into the bargain!

IN SEPARATE BEDROOMS *by Carole Mortimer*

Jack Beauchamp can have any woman he wants – so Mattie Crawford can't understand why he's so determined to take *her* to Paris. Maybe a weekend in the French capital with the best-looking, most charming man she's ever met is his idea of a punishment…

THE ITALIAN'S LOVE-CHILD *by Sharon Kendrick*

Millionaire Luca Cardelli broke Eve's heart years ago, and now he's back. Eve is soon entrapped in the whirlwind of their love affair but her shock is only equalled by Luca's outrageous reaction to some surprising news…

THE GREEK'S VIRGIN BRIDE *by Julia James*

When Andrea Fraser is unexpectedly summoned to Greece she is shocked at the news that awaits her. Her grandfather has found her a husband! Nikos Vassilis may be the most sophisticated man she's ever encountered, but she'll be leaving at the first opportunity – won't she…?

On sale 3rd October 2003

Available at most branches of WHSmith, Tesco, Martins, Borders, Eason, Sainsbury's and all good paperback bookshops.

0903/01a

MILLS & BOON®

Live the emotion

Modern Romance™

THE BILLIONAIRE'S CONTRACT BRIDE by Carol Marinelli

Zavier Chambers is one of Australia's most powerful playboys, and to him Tabitha appears to be the worst kind of woman. Tabitha isn't a gold-digger – but she does need to marry for money. When Zavier blackmails her into marriage she has no choice…

THE TYCOON'S TROPHY MISTRESS by Lee Wilkinson

Daniel Wolfe is not a man to be messed with – and he already has an agenda of his own. Charlotte Michaels soon finds herself being offered an unexpected career move – as her boss's mistress!

THE MARRIAGE RENEWAL by Maggie Cox

When Tara's husband returns after five years, she is willing to give him his divorce – but not until she has told Mac about what happened after he left. Mac is stunned, but he's as consumed with desire for her as he ever was. Is their passion a strong enough basis on which to renew their marriage vows?

MARRIED TO A MARINE by Cathie Linz

Justice Wilder was badly injured while saving a child's life – and now may be facing the end of his military career. Kelly Hart tracks him down in order to convince him to accept help for the first time in his life. But what happens when he discovers she used to love him…?

On sale 3rd October 2003

Available at most branches of WHSmith, Tesco, Martins, Borders, Eason, Sainsbury's and all good paperback bookshops.

0903/01b

MILLS & BOON®

Modern Romance™

...seduction and passion guaranteed

We're on the lookout for HOT new authors...

Think you have what it takes to write a novel?

Then this is your chance!

Can you create:

A proud, passionate and hot-blooded hero that no woman could resist? He has everything – except a woman to share it with...

A sexy and successful contemporary heroine, who can take on the ultimate man on her own terms?

Could you transport readers into a sophisticated international world of tantalizing romantic excitement where seduction and passion are guaranteed?

If so, we want to hear from you!

Visit www.millsandboon.co.uk for editorial guidelines.

Submit the first three chapters and synopsis to:
Harlequin Mills & Boon Editorial Department,
Eton House, 18-24 Paradise Road,
Richmond, Surrey, TW9 1SR,
United Kingdom.

0103/WRITERS/MOD

| books | authors | online reads | magazine | membership |

Visit millsandboon.co.uk and discover your one-stop shop for romance!

Find out everything you want to know about romance novels in one place. Read about and buy our novels online anytime you want.

* Choose and buy books from an extensive selection of Mills & Boon® titles.

* Enjoy top authors and *New York Times* best-selling authors – from Penny Jordan and Miranda Lee to Sandra Marton and Nicola Cornick!

* Take advantage of our amazing **FREE** book offers.

* In our Authors' area find titles currently available from all your favourite authors.

* Get hooked on one of our fabulous online reads, with new chapters updated weekly.

* Check out the fascinating articles in our magazine section.

Visit us online at
www.millsandboon.co.uk

...you'll want to come back again and again!!

WEB/MB

4 BOOKS

AND A SURPRISE GIFT!

We would like to take this opportunity to thank you for reading this Mills & Boon® book by offering you the chance to take FOUR more specially selected titles from the Modern Romance™ series absolutely FREE! We're also making this offer to introduce you to the benefits of the Reader Service™—

   ★ FREE home delivery   ★ FREE gifts and competitions
   ★ FREE monthly Newsletter   ★ Exclusive Reader Service discount
          ★ Books available before they're in the shops

Accepting these FREE books and gift places you under no obligation to buy; you may cancel at any time, even after receiving your free shipment. Simply complete your details below and return the entire page to the address below. *You don't even need a stamp!*

YES! Please send me 4 free Modern Romance™ books and a surprise gift. I understand that unless you hear from me, I will receive 6 superb new titles every month for just £2.60 each, postage and packing free. I am under no obligation to purchase any books and may cancel my subscription at any time. The free books and gift will be mine to keep in any case.

P3ZED

Ms/Mrs/Miss/Mr ....Initials ....
BLOCK CAPITALS PLEASE

Surname ....

Address ....

....

....Postcode ....

Send this whole page to:
UK: FREEPOST CN81, Croydon, CR9 3WZ
EIRE: PO Box 4546, Kilcock, County Kildare (stamp required)

Offer valid in UK and Eire only and not available to current Reader Service subscribers to this series. We reserve the right to refuse an application and applicants must be aged 18 years or over. Only one application per household. Terms and prices subject to change without notice. Offer expires 31st December 2003. As a result of this application, you may receive offers from Harlequin Mills & Boon and other carefully selected companies. If you would prefer not to share in this opportunity please write to The Data Manager at the address above.

Mills & Boon® is a registered trademark owned by Harlequin Mills & Boon Limited.
Modern Romance™ is being used as a trademark.